A Handful of Shadows

Jennifer Hyde

© Jennifer Hyde 1980

Jennifer Hyde has asserted her rights under the Copyright, Design and Patents Act, 1988, to be identified as the author of this work.

First published in 1980 by Woman & Home.

This edition published in 2015 by Endeavour Press Ltd.

Table of Contents

CHAPTER I	5
CHAPTER II	35
CHAPTER III	64
CHAPTER IV	94

CHAPTER I

Descending through the mountain-pierced cloud, the 727 made a perfect landing. Gathering my things, I followed the other passengers—holidaymakers mostly, with a few islanders returning from mainland Portugal—out into the soft, mild evening. Warm, not blindingly hot as it would have been in Greece. Momentarily, my grip tensed on the handrail of the landing steps...but here I was, on Madeira, and I had determined, hadn't I, that there would be absolutely no regrets? Shouldering the rucksack that was my hand luggage, holding my bags and camera, I walked firmly across the tarmac. Twenty minutes later, I was through the formalities of arrival.

Melissa wasn't there. And though I might have expected this in view of the delays in this journey so far, I had to fight off a rising sense of panic. No use telling myself now that I should have waited for an answer to my letter. My fellow passengers drifted away, and I was left stranded amongst the clutter of my luggage, my eyes searching the small airport building for someone—if not Melissa herself, then maybe Felipe Battista, her latest husband.

With a sinking feeling, I realised I could identify no one who might be him, a man admittedly recalled only from a blurred snapshot, heavyish, and with a dark, lugubrious face. There was nothing for it, I would have to find a taxi, blow the cost, and hope it wasn't too far to the Quinta Miranda. I began to look around for a luggage trolley.

'Miss Durrant? Christy Durrant?'

The voice spoke my name from just behind me. I swung round, my smile returning as anxiety fled. 'That's me!' I said happily. It was all right. Of course it was. Melissa wouldn't let me down.

I faced a tall, thin man, his suede jacket slung casually over one shoulder, his hand extended to mine. But his face was cool and unsmiling, unresponsive to my friendliness. His grip was hard and impersonal.

'Battista,' he introduced himself simply, not without a touch of arrogance, in a voice quick with impatience. 'Your flight was so much later than expected, Melissa didn't wait. She was offered a lift home, and you're to drive to the Quinta with me.'

I waited, expecting further elaboration, but none was forthcoming, and though an inexplicable unease stirred in me, I felt a reluctance to ask for explanations of the man before me.

The photo must have been under-exposed, but a certain degree of resemblance to it remained. He wasn't dark at all, though deeply suntanned, making his blond hair a vivid contrast. Moody dark eyes of a curious greyish olive colour, a wide, sensuous mouth, the skin taut across the bones of his face. Younger than I'd expected, possibly a good bit younger than Melissa.

He made no immediate move to go. His eyes appreciatively followed the progress of my pretty stewardess, in her severely-cut, dark green uniform which only served to emphasise her well-developed curves. Feeling all at once travel-jaded and worn out, I eased the jacket from the back of my neck just where the crick of tension was. 'It was good of you to wait for me.'

'Hm?' His gaze swung back. 'Not at all. Less trouble than having to come back again and pick you up.'

It had been a long day, and now this less than enthusiastic reception seemed all of a piece with what the day had done to me. It might have been funny if I'd been less tired. 'There's no answer to that,' I said, and at least it had the effect of rousing him from his own preoccupations.

His glance travelled over me as if aware for the first time that I was there, assessing my feminine potential, which I felt didn't rate all that high at the moment—old jeans, my heavy hair tied carelessly back, looking as I always did when I was tired—heavy-eyed like a drooping child, pale so that there was no disguising the freckles on the bridge of my nose. I felt distinctly grubby, whereas he looked clean and well dressed in a casual, very expensive sort of way.

'Sorry!' he said coolly. 'Didn't mean it to sound quite like that—you'll know what I mean when you see the roads. It's not far to the Quinta but it takes longer than you'd think, with all the twists and turns. Melissa doesn't drive here too often.' He cast a look down at my baggage. 'Is this lot all yours? Good heavens.'

Pushing back a damp strand of hair, I acknowledged the untidy assortment defensively: one small, battered suitcase, heavy; two plastic carrier bags, full to bursting; the tin with Gran's special walnut cake in it;

my rucksack, shoulder bag and camera. Maybe it would have seemed a lot less if I'd been able to use my large suitcase...but that had been borrowed and not returned.

He made no further comment other than a lifted eyebrow, and turned to scan the reception area, a swift, imperious look that immediately summoned up a porter out of thin air, though it surely couldn't be far to the car park.

He himself gingerly picked up one plastic carrier and followed the porter, beckoning me to accompany him with a gesture that was very nearly a command. I did as I was bid, my arm muscles still reminding me how I'd had to lug my own belongings all over Heathrow.

Walking after him, I was conscious of the eyes of every woman in the place following our lordly progression, and knew it wasn't me they were watching. He was eminently watchable, a tall, lean man with a long-legged stride and a distant nonchalance, as if their admiration bored him. Good-looking, and aware of it. That particular brand of careless disdain, his blond hair, his perfect English, that pukka sahib attitude, I thought, skipping a bit to keep up with him...

'You're British, aren't you? Which means you're not Melissa's husband, him being Portuguese and all. So how come you have the same name?'

Momentarily, he slackened speed. 'Melissa's *husband*? What gave you that idea? Surely you've seen photographs and...? No? Well, I'm a sort of cousin of Felipe's. Some of my distant ancestors were Portuguese, but so far back that I'm as English as you are by now. My name's Ben.'

Good news, anyway, that he wasn't, after all, married to Melissa! Ben, not Felipe Battista. Ben— 'Ben Battista!' I exclaimed, only half-believing it.

'I'm beginning to live it down.'

I knew now why his face had seemed familiar. I understood those looks that followed him, and to a certain extent sympathised with his response. Could be he really was sick of adulation.

He was different altogether from his newspaper and magazine photographs and television interviews, maybe simply because he wasn't at this moment smiling the famous Battista smile of daredevil success, his arm round a girl. Invariably, there were girls in Ben Battista's pictures, and usually beautiful ones—sharing champagne drunk out of the Le Mans trophy, posing with him on the steps of a jet. At least, there had been...was it four, five years ago now?

A Handful of Shadows

But what an odd thing, when you thought about it, that Melissa should never have given the tiniest hint that there was any connection between her Felipe and the famous Ben Battista! So utterly unlike her, to keep such an interesting fact to herself.

Again that niggle of worry—because there was no denying that lately Melissa hadn't sounded like her usual self. Her letters had been—unsatisfactory, in a way I couldn't explain. I had shrugged it off, putting it down to overwork for the exhibition she was planning in San Francisco, to her new marriage, or because Melissa was—well, Melissa: my stepmother, so brilliantly talented, with that marvellous gift for creating those delicate, difficult pictures—though that was only one side of the coin.

The other was the volatile temperament that seemed to turn in on itself, to become a negative force when it came to coping with her emotional problems. She was now on her third husband, and hadn't made a conspicuous success of the previous two, the first being my father. I hadn't realised this last until after my father's death. I had always adored her, depended on her for love and affection as well as support and encouragement whenever I needed it. There'd never been a time when she hadn't given it to me, even through the years of separation, even if it had to be by letter, or telephone.

For the first time in my headlong rush to her, it occurred to me to wonder—could it be possible that now, just when I needed her most, Melissa was going to fail me?

*

The air moved, as soft as silk, around me as I stood waiting by the sporty white Alfa Romeo until my luggage was stowed, and the porter had departed, his huge grin evidently reflecting the size of his tip. Ben Battista saw me strapped into my seat and walked round to open his door, slung his beautiful jacket on to the back seat and slid into the low-slung driving position with a cautious, easing movement.

He quickly intercepted my enquiring look. 'No problem when I'm behind the wheel, it's just getting there that does it,' he said.

Glancing in the mirror, he let in the clutch smoothly so that the car shot forward, fast and sure as an oiled bolt. He was getting over an accident, he added; nothing much, but his back still needed treating with respect when bending and lifting, that sort of thing.

'Still? After all these years?'

A car was approaching fast along the main road and he drew to a halt at the T-junction. 'Not that accident,' he said unemotionally. 'More recently.'

A car roared past in the direction of Funchal, a dark green, open-topped MGB, with a girl at the wheel. She turned her head and raised an arm in greeting as she flashed by, black hair streaming, her scarf a bright orange banner behind her.

'Caterina Duente,' he remarked, returning the wave. 'The daughter of the neighbour who took Melissa home.'

Half my mind registered the warmth in his voice, whilst the other half was occupied with the fact that I'd evidently been doing him an injustice, thinking him too high and mighty to carry my luggage himself. Something in his attitude ought to have warned me that he wasn't the sort to take kindly to sympathy, but as usual, I didn't stop to think twice before I spoke. 'I'm sorry about your back—should you be driving at all?'

'Don't worry about it, you're safe enough with me!'

'No, no, that wasn't what I meant! I just thought it might still be a bit dicey for you. A pity, after getting over that other accident so fantastically.'

'That was four years ago.' There was no mistaking the edge to his voice, now. 'You disappoint me. I didn't think you'd be the type, Miss Durrant.'

'Christy, for goodness' sake! And what type?' I asked, intrigued to know into which category he slotted me—though wasn't his judgment a bit premature.

'The "Oh-Mr-Battista-I-think-you're-wonderful" type. Nothing, I assure you, is more boring. I had an accident, I got better. End of story.' When I hadn't replied for several moments, he sighed. 'Now you're offended.'

'I don't offend that easily.' Which was true, but might, I felt, have been forgivable in the circumstances. He'd simply rendered me speechless, not an easy thing for anyone to accomplish. 'Nor impress easily, either,' I added.

He gave a grunt that might have been a laugh. 'OK, I'm sorry—though you might take it as a compliment if you knew me better. I'm really only rotten to my friends.'

'In that case, I accept your apology, Mr Battista.'

'Ben to my friends, Christy.'

A glance at his profile showed maybe the faintest trace of an answering smile, but after that his monosyllabic replies discouraged my further attempts at conversation. I took the hint, sinking back into the unaccustomed luxury of the chocolate brown leather interior of the car, allowing myself to drink in first impressions of the island as we headed into a Technicolor sunset.

He drove the car swiftly, effortlessly, sliding it like a fish round the narrow hairpin bends of the road, with its countless passing places, that hugged the coastline. Rising on the other side was a series of thickly forested peaks, split with deeply-cut ravines. We passed a church with an odd, onion-shaped dome, clinging to the slope, occasional houses and villas, Portuguese style, softly colour-washed, with red tiled roofs and stepped gardens.

Every kind of creeper spilled over walls, roofs and terraces in almost indecent profusion, a rainbow blaze of purple, scarlet, yellow. It seemed too theatrical to be quite real. I felt an upsurge of pure pleasure, already more than half under the spell of this small island, this submerged volcano rising from the sea. Whatever might turn out, to spend time in such a tourist paradise couldn't be bad.

Though I was scarcely a tourist, and this wasn't exactly a holiday. But just like all the other holidaymakers, I would soon be gone. Back to England, and Dave, returned from Greece. The thought should have cheered me. I was depressed to find it didn't.

I began to wish the man beside me would make some effort at the polite small talk that usually smoothed the path between strangers. It wouldn't have been difficult. After all, everything was new to me, and I was ready with a thousand questions about the island, and where we were going. Above all, I would have liked to talk about Melissa. But here, something held me back. Despite the slight rise in temperature between us which followed our small exchange, there was something that prevented me from being at ease with him, that didn't fit the easy-going, playboy image his famous name conjured up, something reserved and self-contained to the point of being daunting.

He braked and changed gear, slowing down to pass two barefoot children ahead, with large bundles, partly covered with broad shiny leaves, balanced on their heads. When they heard the car approaching, they drew into the side of the road, waving, their round brown faces lit with laughter.

'Are those bananas they're carrying?' I asked.

'Sure. Those are Felipe's plantations down there.' He pointed to what looked like a flat strip of land, below the road, and as we reached the children, he waved and smiled back at them. A real smile this time, white teeth vivid against his tanned skin.

And there it was, the face I remembered. Mr Dream-boat himself.

I tried to recall what I'd read about the spectacular racing crash that had made headlines the world over. He had almost died, hadn't he, when his car had left the track and burst into flames? A typically cool Battista gesture, said the Press, praising him for his skill in avoiding a pile-up with other drivers. They said, too, it was only his iron will that had pulled him through. Looking at the stubborn set of his jaw, the profile of his thin, tense face, I found no difficulty in believing that. This man would never knuckle under, would always fight.

Then I remembered his subsequent decision to retire from racing. He would give no explanation, no interviews, and sane and sensible though the decision might have been, it wasn't the stuff out of which the media could make heroes or headlines. The racing world had lost a colourful, extrovert personality, every schoolboy's idol, every woman's heart-throb.

Wait a minute, though. There had been something else. I sat twiddling a strand of hair, a subconscious habit I had in moments of stress or concentration, and let it go when I realised what I was doing. It hadn't helped as a memory aid, anyway. Whatever it was remained stubbornly submerged between the layers of my mind.

Our route had turned inland, towards the lonely heartland of the island, and signs of habitation had virtually disappeared. The road was even narrower than the coast road. It began curling upwards in a succession of incredible S-bends, twisting at what appeared to be an almost vertical gradient, with dizzy-making drops suddenly appearing at the side. The afterglow had left the sky, and the peaks began to look lonely and desolate, and I shivered as the car thrust bumpily upwards.

He switched on the headlights, and they glowed redly on the trunks of pines. 'Relax,' he said suddenly, 'there's nothing to be afraid of.'

'Oh, I'm not frightened.'

'Good.' But after my fairly obvious lie, he roused himself to point out that the road, after passing Melissa's house and its two neighbours, went only to the volcanic centre of the island, stopping at a vantage point where the views were spectacular. 'So it's quite safe. Any tourist bus or car will have left by now,' he added, 'though it's not a road for the dark, even when you know it well.'

'I can believe that! But that expedition sounds like a must on my list of things to see. Perhaps Melissa will take me.'

Not so much as by the flicker of an eyelid did he give any indication that I'd said the wrong thing, yet the tension gathering in him vibrated tangibly, communicating to me so that I felt I must unwittingly have touched him on the raw again.

I had only a moment to wonder what on earth it could be this time before he answered calmly enough. 'No need to bother Melissa—if you want to go, I'll take you. Any time, just ask.'

'Well, thanks. That's very kind of you.'

'It'll be a pleasure,' he said automatically. 'How long do you intend staying here, by the way?'

'Depends on Melissa. A couple of months, I suppose, at least until … '

'Until what?' I sensed a sudden focusing of attention on me, a shift of interest as though his great indifference had at last been pierced. Before I'd found an answer, he was saying, 'I wonder how likely you are to take advice?'

'That usually means something unpalatable! But why don't you try me and see?'

'Two months is a long time. Why don't you have your holiday, a fortnight or whatever, and then go home? Believe me,' he said, disapproval strong in his voice, 'it would be better for you, for—everyone, if you didn't stay longer. Things have a habit of turning sour if you overdo them.'

His words sent a ripple of shock and puzzlement through me. We were still ascending, so high now that the road was misty with cloud vapour. I was still searching for an answer when we came through it. He sighed. 'I thought you might take it that way, though it was only meant for your own good—and Melissa's.'

'Melissa's?' I said coldly. 'I'm afraid I'm not with you.'

'Let's be frank, then. I think she's in no state at the moment to have neurotic stepdaughters crying on her shoulder.'

Maybe the shock was less, after the previous one. But it still hurt. Especially since it had a basis of truth. He drove the knife deeper. 'That's what you're here for, isn't it?'

It wasn't like that at all. I needed Melissa, it was true, but I wasn't running away—I was not! I supposed Melissa had read him my letter and he had interpreted it in his own unsympathetic way.

I turned my face to hide its giveaway expression. When I saw the drop at the side, I wished I hadn't, and turned quickly back. And he was saying, 'This is my day for putting my foot in it! I suppose you think that's something I'd absolutely no right to say?'

'Please forget it.'

But he said soberly, 'I'm an edgy so-and-so at the best of times, and I've had quite a day today, what with one thing and another. The affair with Melissa at the airport was the last straw, but that's no excuse for taking it out on you. I really am sorry—can you forgive me?'

'Please—everyone says things they wish they hadn't.'

I conceded his ownership of a bad temper; in fact it brought him right off his pedestal down to my own level, and he really did sound contrite. But I couldn't help wondering how far the charm was genuine, how far it was deliberately switched on—and try as I might, I couldn't forgive as immediately as all that, when his words brought back everything I was trying to come to terms with.

My tutors at university had thought me distressingly light-hearted and high-spirited, and maybe they'd been right, because it had been fun, those years at college. Between the parties and the meaningful discussions on Life, I'd made a host of new friends, learned how to manage my own resources, become independent. I'd fallen lightly in love a few times—and then, with Dave.

Only, too late, I realised I hadn't put in enough work. I'd scraped through, but my results were not nearly as good as they should have been. My self-confidence was shattered. Still, I was Christy, the girl known for meeting life with a laugh, and I attempted to joke it off, as a lot of others did.

Then followed the months of job-hunting, taking temporary work while I angled and hoped for that one particular job I really wanted, the feather I so desperately needed to adorn my cap. Only I hadn't got it. A week ago I'd finally heard that I'd been turned down.

'Should it be of interest to you, I've absolutely no intention of crying on anyone's shoulder. I just need some time to get my bearings, then I'm quite sure I'll find myself a super job,' I told Ben Battista now, recklessly, and without any basis yet for certainty.

Unexpectedly, he laughed. 'That's the spirit! But as a matter of interest, just why have you come here?'

'Do I have to have a reason for visiting Melissa?'

'No-o. But she's asked you to come before, hasn't she, and you never would.'

Not because I hadn't wanted to, but because there had never before been the money available for expensive trips to Madeira, but I didn't say that aloud. You didn't, not to someone who had probably never wanted for a thing in his life. How could he have understood what it was like, trying to scrape together every penny for the air fare?

The small legacy from my godmother couldn't have arrived at a better time for me. Almost immediately, with an enormous sense of relief, I had known what I was going to do with it.

Go to Madeira. That was it. Melissa would help me sort myself out, soothe my wounded pride as she'd kissed me better when I'd bumped myself as a child. Melissa would know just what I ought to do, she always had. The letter was sent, my ticket bought and my headlong journey started without waiting for a reply, so sure had I been of her welcome.

Dave had been predictably furious at what I'd done. 'You can't go! You've already promised to come to Greece!'

'I know, and I'm sorry, Dave, I really am.'

It was true that I was sorry. It would have been tremendous fun, the seven of us, packing camping gear and Dave's guitar into the old converted van we'd borrowed, setting off on a shoestring for the hot sun, the wine and the magic of the Greek islands.

'It's not as though you'll be going alone, though,' I reminded him, and thought of Tanya Simpson.

'It won't be the same.'

He'd argued endlessly with me, until he realised I wasn't going to be put off, that I meant what I said. And then he'd been so sick about it, he'd refused to speak to me for ages.

'Well, go if you must,' he said finally, 'but don't expect me to hang around for ever.'

I think it was at that point I first admitted to myself that things might not be going to work out between us. It was fairly obvious what he'd been hoping for from the Greek holiday, but I wasn't going to commit myself to that sort of relationship, not with Dave, not with anyone, yet.

So they'd set off without me, and now it seemed as though my presence here wasn't going to be welcomed much either, since Melissa had gone off without bothering to wait for me. And Ben Battista was warning me off, too. I felt that dreary sense of foreboding that lies like a lump somewhere around the midriff.

I said slowly, 'What was that you said about Melissa just now? Did something dire happen at the airport?'

'Oh, that. She passed out, fainted.' He frowned. 'Luckily, Senhor Duente, who lives over there—' he gave a jerk of his head to the right— 'had just flown in, so I persuaded her to let him drive her home.'

'Fainted?' I sat very still. Yet in a way, it was almost a relief to find there might be a physical explanation for her untypical behaviour. 'She's ill?'

'Not so far as I know. She passed out because I gather she hadn't eaten a thing all day.'

'But she never did eat much.' Not enough to keep a sparrow alive, Gran used to say.

'And not much yesterday either, I suspect, or the day before.'

Well, not even Melissa was that absent-minded. All my unsubstantiated fears came rushing together. I felt a constriction in my throat as I asked, 'Why? Is there something worrying her?'

He hunched himself nearer the steering wheel. 'She's not talking about it to anyone, if there is.'

But he knew all right, I was sure of it. Carefully, as though I trod on eggs, I asked, 'Something to do with Felipe?'

He didn't answer immediately, occupying himself by turning the car into a short, steep and overgrown drive, parking it with familiarity into a space in which it just fitted. Incongruously, next to it was a battered green Ford which seemed all the same more suited to the island roads.

Before getting out, he rolled down his window, leaning his elbow out and half-turning to me, giving me a long, appraising look. 'See what I mean? Already you're putting two and two together. Has it occurred to you, you might just come up with the wrong answers? And in any case, it's nothing to do with either you or me.'

This time he robbed the words of offence by his smile, and though I suspected he might be using his attractiveness for deliberate effect, I found I was smiling back, warmed and responsive despite myself. And this very thing, and the touch of his hand on mine as he gave it a short sharp squeeze to emphasise his words, put me immediately on guard and challenged me, made my decision: I would be neither intimidated nor disarmed by him.

'So you're staying here, too?' I asked, watching him lock the Alfa, though I might have worked that one out for myself.

'I live here. I have a chalet in the garden, further up the hill.'

The breeze brought with it an overpowering fragrance, sickly in its intensity, which increased as we climbed the drive to the house. The last quarter of the moon had risen, and the Quinta Miranda had a strange abandoned air in its light, a discarded doll's house that had been carelessly tossed aside and landed accidentally against the side of the towering hill; a largish, shabby building with many verandas and a shallow, pantiled roof.

There was a sound of rushing water above the soughing of the trees, and he brushed away a predatory branch of sagging creeper that stretched tentacles towards us as we went up the steps. The stucco, which might once have been pink, was peeling, and the heavy carved door was dried and granulated by the weather.

There were no welcoming lights at any of the windows. Somewhere, a shutter banged interminably.

From inside the house came the high yapping of a dog. I would have recognised Heathcliff's hysterical barking anywhere. Heathcliff! I remembered so well the day my father had brought home the small, bad-tempered Yorkshire terrier as a present for Melissa. It was only later when I was old enough to read *Wuthering Heights* that I understood the joke about his name...I'm not sure my father ever really did appreciate it.

A light went on at a front window, quick tapping footsteps approached. I felt myself braced to face any unwillingness to welcome me, but I needn't have worried. The door flew open into a dark, shadowed hall lit dimly by a single lamp at the far end, and there was Melissa, poised like a wisp of thistledown, as if a sudden breeze might blow her away. A moment of wariness, a moment only, then—

'Christy, angel!'

Her light, breathy voice was vibrant with emotion; her scent, that well-remembered, tantalising fragrance, surrounded me as we flew into one another's arms, whilst Heathcliff danced around our feet, snapping at me in such an excess of jealousy that she had to order him to be quiet.

'He's forgotten you, but he'll soon get used to you again,' she laughed, standing back, inspecting me at arm's length. 'You've grown up,' she announced, hugging me again.

I had always known that pale air of fragility was deceptive, that underneath she was competent and tough, her nature extrovert and happy, full of an infectious zest for living. Now, however, my certainty had been shaken, and I searched anxiously for signs to reassure myself. I was infinitely relieved to find no outward cause for alarm.

She was nudging forty, and she was in no way beautiful, but she had style, her high cheekbones accentuating the delicate modelling of her face, her light brown hair fashionably unruly. She was wearing a long loose dress with a halter neckline that left her arms and shoulders bare. It looked like a couture model. She had probably made it herself.

I'd been taller than her since I was fourteen, and now, beside her sophisticated china-boned five foot nothing, I felt myself back in adolescence, quite likely to bump into furniture and drop things. 'Not surprising I've changed, it's four years since you saw me,' I reminded her, gauche with inexplicable shyness, as I remembered that last flying visit she'd made from America to see Gran and me. Where had all the years gone?

Melissa turned quickly and took the hand of a tall woman who had come into the hall, drawing her forward to meet me.

'Dee, this is Christy, here after all this time. You've both heard about each other, haven't you, from your wicked stepmother?' she laughed.

Dee Newman, technically Melissa's other stepdaughter, was in fact just a few years younger than Melissa herself, maybe thirty-seven or eight. She took my hand in a firm, warm clasp, and her own hands, I noticed, were shapely and ringless.

'I'm so glad to see you here at last, my dear.' Her voice was pleasant and cultured, with overtones of New England, her face calm and full of repose, her eyes of an unusual clear golden-amber, with a deep way of looking at you. 'We must have some long talks and get to know each other. Right now, though, I'd best fix you some food. I guess you must be hungry. You and Melissa can do all your talking over dinner.'

She went out as quietly as she had come in, and Ben looked at his watch. 'If you women are going to make up for lost time, I'll leave you to it—unless you'd prefer me to stay?' he asked, bestowing an enquiring concerned look on Melissa. 'I will if you want me to.'

'Of course not! Now Christy's here, everything will be fine. I know you've things to do—and I've given you a ghastly time already today, haven't I?'

'No more than usual.' He grinned, then with returning seriousness, added, 'But it's as well Duente was there to bring you back.'

Her eyes lost a little of their blue brilliance, her hands made small nervous flutters so that the heavily-laden gold seal bracelet on her wrist jangled. She gave him an odd little look I couldn't fathom. 'I'd much rather have stayed with you and waited.'

'It was only sensible to come home. You look much better. Now, sure you'll be all right?'

He took both her small, restless hands and held them calmingly between his own brown ones. I saw a tenderness softening the taut planes of his face, which at first surprised, then angered me.

'Quite sure, Ben dear. And thank you again for—everything.'

She stood on tiptoe, the deep blue dress falling in sculptured folds to the ground, holding her face upwards, flower-like, for the light kiss he bent to place on her lips. I caught a reflection in a long mirror on the opposite wall...Dee, standing motionless in the doorway. As Ben said good night, Dee walked forward to the front door and held it open for him. Her own low good night to him was reserved and cool, her face shuttered.

The whole spectacle had been quite sickening, I agreed, making my own farewells to him as brief as possible. I was annoyed at the strength of my reactions, furious with him for playing on Melissa's ready emotions, and, at the same time, hoping quite desperately that the whole mad merry-go-round wasn't starting again.

The first time Melissa married, it had been to my father, when he was already a widower with me, his eight-year-old daughter. My mother had died when I was born, and my grandmother had come to live with us, keeping house and bringing me up.

Melissa's arrival had changed my life. She brought into our quiet, staid household in a little Kentish village another dimension of excitement and variety. She taught the small, serious child I had been to laugh and lose my reserve, forging a strong bond between us that brought us closer perhaps, in its way, than mother and daughter. But I never thought of her as a mother, more as an elder sister, a friend. It was a terrible shock to me when, a few months after my father's death, she had announced her intention of leaving me and going to work in the United States.

'I *must* go, darling—alone. I need to be on the move, to find some new experience for my work, a new landscape. It hasn't been growing as it should, not for years, don't you see? But it won't be any sort of life for a fourteen-year-old. There's your schooling for one thing. You need to live in a settled home, you'll be better here, with Gran...and of course, I'll come back to visit you.'

Gran was wiser than I. 'I'm a great believer in holding on to the ones you love by letting them go,' she told me. It was small comfort, but it was impossible to go on feeling resentful when Melissa's long and loving letters constantly assured me that I wasn't forgotten, that we'd soon be together again; and when her few visits coloured my life so warmly.

It hadn't occurred to me until I was much older that Melissa's marriage to my father might not have been ideal. To me, he'd been wise, loving and generous, but afterwards, little things came back to me. I began to realise his devoted anxiety for her had not been enough, that the dull, cherished years as his wife had been utterly restricting for one of her butterfly temperament and talents. Her work was revitalised, took off, after she left England.

Within a few years her reputation had grown, her work was selling well. Life was wonderful, she reported. Then, quite out of the blue, she had married again, this time to Oliver Newman, the wealthy art dealer and entrepreneur who had acted as her agent, promoted her exhibitions and so on, a man more than twenty years her senior. I never met him. The marriage had ended with his sudden death, here on Madeira, two years ago, with Melissa left a rich woman, and owner of this house.

Long before that, however, there had been indications that all was not well with them. Towards the end, Oliver was scarcely mentioned in her letters. All the same, his death had evidently been a shock to her. When she'd flown home for an unexpected couple of days to attend to some business in England, she'd been in a state of nervous tension that had bordered on breakdown, Gran confided to me. By then I'd been at college, and I grieved to have missed her flying visit.

'I begged her to think of coming home again to live,' Gran had said. 'I hate to think of her being there all alone—but she wouldn't listen.'

'Madeira's my home now,' Melissa had replied, and it was with mixed feelings that we heard within a few months that she was to be married for the third time, this time to Felipe Battista, owner of a banana plantation. Once more she was in love, truly in love, we must visit her and Felipe, we could see how happy she was! Had she discovered afresh that marriage wasn't all a bed of roses? She'd talked non-stop since my arrival, but it was all surface chat, telling little of herself, almost as if she were afraid to plunge deeper. She was smiling, cheerful, but brittle as eggshells.

A Handful of Shadows

*

We sat together now over a prolonged meal in the dining-room, a shadowed room, oppressive with dark mahogany and an unattractive brownish wallpaper that seemed an unhappy choice for the smiling climate of Madeira. For all the sparkling cleanliness and polish, it was a strange house altogether. There was something wrong in the atmosphere…I traced the pattern of the embroidery on my place mat, trying to work out what it was.

'Aren't they lovely, the mats?' Melissa said.

I bent to examine them more closely—linen exquisitely embroidered in cut work—glad to be able to throw off my uneasy thoughts, to be able to admire something with genuine enthusiasm, while Melissa explained the embroidery was the work of local women.

'They do it in their cottages, and then it's taken down to Funchal to be packaged and marketed. Felipe had an idea of going into that line, but —' She broke off, shrugging. 'Christy, I'm longing for you to meet him, but this wretched business appointment …'

Her voice trailed off again. For perhaps the tenth time, she looked at her watch, then gave a small, almost imperceptible sigh. 'After eleven. He won't be home tonight, not now. He'll stay overnight in Funchal and go straight to the office from there.'

The overhead lamp was harsh. I saw that I'd been mistaken in thinking her unchanged. There were threads of grey in her hair, the light sharpened the hollows of her face, robbed her skin of its glow, and showed a glitter than might conceivably have been tears in her eyes; but after that she became more relaxed.

'Does Felipe often have to leave you alone like this?' I asked.

She smiled brightly. 'I'm hardly alone, am I? I have Dee, and Ben's only a few steps away; I've only to call on him if I need.'

I made a non-committal sound, concentrating on the food on my plate. It was delicious, some sort of fish in a rich, creamy sauce, brought in by a young, merry-faced girl called Josefina. Dee hadn't joined us, pleading a slight headache.

'And there's tact for you,' Melissa said. 'Leaving us alone on your first night here.'

'She's nice, isn't she?'

'Wonderful. She has such a quiet strength, I really don't know how I ever managed without her. She was with us when her father—when Oliver—

died.' She paused for the space of a second, absorbed in some private vision of her own. 'Afterwards, she actually gave up her apartment in Boston and came to live here with me. She offered to leave when Felipe and I got married, but we both wanted her to stay—she's such a help and comfort. Not that we haven't got a splendid house-keeper in Marian Lopes. You'll have realised Marian's English?'

'The woman who took my cases upstairs? How does she come to be out here?'

'She's the widow of a Madeira man, and she was Felipe's housekeeper for years before we married. She has two little boys, looked after by an aunt in Funchal, and she spends the weekends with them. Dee sort of takes over here then—during the week she has a part-time job as Duente's secretary—and she also types out the final draft of Ben's manuscripts.'

'Manuscripts? What sort of manuscripts?'

'Angel, he's Ben McLeod!' she paused with fine dramatic intent, waiting for me to be impressed. I searched my memory without success, and she looked disappointed.

'Well, I don't suppose his books feature on university reading lists—they're thrillers with a motor racing background and, I tell you, they're a wow. Fancy never having heard of them, though. You've been leading too cloistered an existence, chick!'

I dabbed at crumbs of bread with my forefinger, then licked them off. Was it true my life was narrow? I thought for an instant of the years since my father's death, bounded by the confines of school, then college, dominated recently by little other than the demands of my absorbed relationship with Dave. 'Maybe you're right,' I admitted.

'I have all three of his books,' Melissa went on, giving me a shrewd glance. 'You must read them while you're here. I promise you won't be bored.'

'I can't wait,' I told her truthfully, mentally according Ben Battista respect. Two careers, both of them successful, and he couldn't be more than thirty, if that.

Melissa said, 'Dee's just finished typing his last book, which is lucky for him, because Duente has some work that's going to keep her busy from now on. He's a wine exporter, but he has his finger in most of the island pies. I can't think how she stands working for him—he's perfectly beastly to her.'

Unaccountably, she shivered, as if a goose had walked over her grave, and drained her glass at a gulp.

'What's his daughter like?' I asked. 'We caught a glimpse of her on the way here.'

'Caterina?' Melissa wrinkled her nose. 'All right, if you like the type. Pretty, dresses well — I shouldn't think you'd have much in common.'

'Oh, thanks!'

We laughed together. 'You know what I mean! Anyway, you'd beat her hands down if you took the trouble—oh help, I'm making it worse, aren't I? But her father spoils her—her mother died years ago—and well, frankly...Still, you're bound to meet her and draw your own conclusions. There are only the three houses around here—ours, the Duentes' and the clinic. Ben seems to get on all right with her,' she added inconsequently.

'He does?'

Melissa shook her head as I offered her more sauce. I helped myself to some and she watched me spoon it on my plate. She said suddenly, 'You and Ben didn't hit it off, did you?'

'I shouldn't think we're exactly fated to be soul-mates.'

'Funny, I'd have thought you and he...'

'Don't! To begin with, I don't go for the scalp-hunting type...'

She interrupted, quite sharply. 'You don't want to believe everything you read in the papers, Christy. Ben's not in the least like that. He's been a very good friend to me, he's kind and reliable, a darling really.'

'He has a weird way of showing it. He hardly spoke to me on the way here, except to be disagreeable.'

'Poor old you! I have to admit he was a bit uptight earlier on, when things went haywire while we were waiting for you—but you know, I sometimes wonder if he isn't still in pain.'

'He said he'd had an accident recently.' I was still curious about that. 'What happened?'

'Something to do with the helter-skelter, which did him no good at all, as you may imagine.'

'The what?'

'The slide in the children's playground at the clinic. He's always over there, for one reason or another.' A slight note of disapproval crept into her voice. 'Have some more wine,' she offered, pouring herself a third glass as I declined more.

'No, thanks. You've scarcely eaten anything,' I reminded her, feeling like somebody's nanny, as she pushed her plate away almost untouched, then reached for a cigarette. 'And that can't be very intelligent, can it, after what happened at the airport?'

'Oh, please don't, there's a love. Ben made me drink some soup after I did that Sarah Bernhardt thing—all highly dramatic, wasn't it?—and it succeeded in taking away any appetite I might have had.'

'Well, if you've had something…'

I tried to turn a cracking yawn into a smile, but Melissa didn't appear to notice my tiredness, despite the fact that she was leaning forward on her elbows, studying me intently.

'I used to think you'd grow up looking like that picture of your mother, but you haven't, not in the least.'

'I know.' I laughed regretfully, but not very. I'd long ago come to terms with that. 'I'm never going to be Miss World, am I?'

'You have something else, though. A sort of glow that shines from you, as if laughter and happiness weren't ever very far away.' She was watching me, brooding. 'Still young enough to blush, you make me feel a thousand years old—how I envy you!' Then with an unexpectedness that astonished me, her face quickened. It was a look I'd seen too many times to be mistaken, the rush of creative joy that animated her, filled her small, frail being with purpose and intent.

But when she spoke, I hadn't expected what came. 'Paint *me*?' I repeated.

Her soft, breathy voice sharpened to urgency. 'I haven't ever done much with portraits, as you know—but you've given me an idea. With that creamy skin and all that electric bronze hair—it's gorgeous with your hazel eyes—possibly I could give you a sort of Burne-Jones mediaeval background, hm?' Head on one side, she considered me. 'Maybe not. Maybe—anyway, will you, Christy?'

I could do no other than agree.

'This may be absolutely what I've been needing, a different approach—something *new*,' she went on. 'You see, Christy…oh, love, I *am* sorry! We've got weeks ahead, and really, you look half dead. You must be simply aching for bed.'

Sensing too late that she had been on the brink of a confidence, I cursed the yawn that had overtaken me, but I was just about dropping in my tracks. I pushed back my chair. 'Are you coming, too?'

'Oh, I'll be up later.' The air of excitement was still vibrant about her. 'I may even sketch one or two preliminary ideas.' She bent and plucked up Heathcliff. 'Sleep well.' She gave me a kiss and a long look, then touching my cheek lightly, she said, 'I haven't liked to ask you—but are you very unhappy, poor love? About you know what?'

'Losing that job? Not unhappy exactly; unsure. I'm all in a muddle, Melissa.'

'Well, if you want to talk about it, just say the word. Otherwise I won't mention it again. I know how tiresome folks can be when they go on and on.'

I blessed her for her understanding as I went upstairs. The floorboards creaked as I crossed the floor of my room, its French windows open to a tiny balcony. The dominant face of the rocky hillside seemed to rise abruptly in front of me, looming in the moonlight to an enormous height, its dense bulk overpowering the house. I was glad to lower the louvred shutters and blank it out.

I was too tired even to unpack, but my clothes weren't on the whole likely to be spoiled by a night in a suitcase. Before I got into bed, however, I took out the framed photograph of Dave and put it on the bedside table.

I wondered what they were doing, my friends, and whether Dave was thinking of me. I tried to picture him on the beach at Delos, but couldn't. When I turned out the light, a tense, masculine face with deep-set eyes, as familiar as if I'd known it for years, superimposed itself on my inner eye.

The bed was unfamiliar and the wind moaned with a softly mournful whine, but I doubted whether either would keep me awake. They didn't. Not until the small hours of the morning, when the wind woke me with its low keening, an insistent, repetitive sound that was eerily like a woman sobbing. Or was it the wind? If it had been, it stopped a moment after I clicked on the bedside lamp to see that the time was around two in the morning. For a long time after I'd switched it off again, I lay trying to fight off the sense of wretchedness the sobbing sound had aroused in me, trying not to remember that the nearest room to mine was Melissa's.

*

I slept the clock round, waking to the sound of tumbling water, which brought me from my bed to pad across the floorboards in bare feet. Raising the shutters on a milky blue sky feathered with cloud, I stepped out on to the balcony. The sight took away my breath.

The tremendous cliff-like hillside, which last night had seemed menacing, again rose before me—but now the dense, impenetrable evergreen growth that clothed it seemed only to form a perfect backdrop for the narrow strip of garden which separated it from the back of the house.

A river of blue morning glory poured over a trellis, purple bougainvillaea flaunted against an adjacent wing of the house. Beyond was the deep inviting green of feathery palms and shrubs, a glimpse of a narrow stream of bright falling water, a shimmer of light on a pool. And over all, that heavy, cloying scent I'd noticed last night. My spirits lifted. I went to rummage in my case for a cotton wrap and slippers, had a quick wash at the old-fashioned jug and basin arrangement in the corner and ran a brush through my tangled hair until it crackled.

No one was about as I went down the curving staircase, trailing my hand on the polished wood of the banister. The black and white chequered floor of the dim hall was still damp from washing, and I saw through the open door that if anyone had eaten breakfast in the dining-room, the table had been cleared and not re-laid.

A delicious, mouth-watering smell of fresh coffee and hot bread drew me towards the kitchen. Young Josefina, in a short-sleeved white blouse and voluminous apron, her black plaits, neatly coiled round her head, was at the sink, preparing vegetables. As I came in, she turned to greet me with her wide, happy smile.

The housekeeper, Marian Lopes, was also there. She looked up from taking a tray of small round cakes from the oven, a stocky woman wearing a nylon overall that echoed the pale blue of her eyes. She offered me a terse good morning. 'I'll get you your breakfast in a minute.'

'No rush, Mrs Lopes.'

'Unless you'd rather bath first? There's water today,' she said obscurely, and without waiting for my reply she added, 'And you might as well call me Marian. Everybody else does.'

She spoke with a marked north-country accent but despite the invitation to informality, her manner was anything but friendly. Tucking back a strand of faded hair from a broad forehead, she began deftly shaping more of the small cakes for the oven. 'If you wait till I've finished these, I'll serve you your breakfast out on the terrace.'

'Oh, please don't bother. I'll get it myself.'

She looked coolly disapproving. 'It'll be no trouble,' she said, managing to convey that it would, but that other alternatives wouldn't be acceptable, either. I sensed the strong, imposing will of a stubborn woman, and something in me resisted the idea of knuckling under, even in such a small thing.

'If I could just have a cup of coffee,' I insisted, heading firmly for the bubbling percolator.

Marian's lips tightened, but she signalled Josefina to bring me a plate of the cakes and butter and a thick earthenware cup and saucer. She then put the fresh batch of cakes into the oven, rubbed her hands on a towel and, after saying something to Josefina in her own language, went out. Josefina and I exchanged smiles. I sat down to eat at the kitchen table and Josefina leaned against the sink, prepared to talk.

It wasn't necessary, as I feared, to use sign language. Josefina could make herself understood quite well in English. We got along fine. I learned that Marian Lopes and Josefina between them coped with the cooking and the cleaning—but not to forget Emilio, Josefina added, rosy-faced, he who did the garden. She informed me that Dee would soon be leaving for work at the Duente house, and that Melissa was already working this morning. She took me to the window and pointed out a path winding upwards to a small building, red-roofed, nestling amongst the trees.

'The senhora's studio?' I asked.

'*Nâo, nâo!*' She shook her head vehemently. That was the *cabine* belonging to Senhor Ben. I must go near there, then I would see the studio.

Thanking her for my breakfast, I was about to go and seek out my bath when the door opened and Dee came in, carrying a used breakfast tray, with Marian Lopes at her heels. '*Bom dia*, Josefina. Good morning, Christy. I hope you slept well.'

The headache of the previous evening, if real, seemed to have disappeared. She looked crisp, composed and efficient; she threw a swift, comprehensive glance round the kitchen and evidently noted that everything was in order. Marian marched over to the oven and took out the last batch of cakes.

Dee turned to me and asked me what my plans for the day were. 'I'm afraid you're going to be left to your own devices. Melissa appears to be working and I too, today, which means I must take the car. I have to run into Funchal for Senhor Duente. Mostly, I use it, since Melissa doesn't drive much.'

Twice I'd been told that. 'She used to love driving—fast,' I remarked. 'Too fast, sometimes.'

'That's just it—she can't stand driving sedately, and you must have seen for yourself how dangerous the roads round here can be.'

I told her I'd heard there was plenty of good walking, so I shouldn't be at a loss as to how to spend my time. She said quickly, 'Don't go too far, and keep to the roads. Walking in these mountains can be more dangerous than driving—and don't forget to take warm clothing. It's often bitterly cold up there.'

'I'll promise to take my survival kit! I belonged to a rambling club at college, so I'm used to walking.' Though not in the mountains, not with my head for heights.

'Nevertheless, when the *capacete* comes down—that's the cloud cap which hangs over the tops—even experienced people would hesitate about tackling some of the climbs without a guide.'

'No one but a fool would wander about in the mist—not unless they were deliberately asking for trouble,' I said cheerfully.

Behind us there was a sudden clatter, and Josefina threw a frightened look at Dee before kneeling to pick up the baking tray she had knocked off the table with her elbow.

Marian said, roughly but not unkindly, 'Get on with your work, girl. I'll pick this up myself.' She knelt down, her face hidden as she bent over the mess of crumbs.

Dee took my arm and, with a quick gesture, drew me through the kitchen door into the hall. Even in that dim light, I could see that she was distressed, her face very pale.

'Christy, I don't believe you'd ever be deliberately malicious—but…is it possible that Melissa hasn't told you?'

'Told me what?'

'About my father. No, I see she hasn't. My dear, he died in just such circumstances. He was walking on the Pico do Aeriero when the mist came down. They didn't find his body until next day, a thousand feet below.'

Shock momentarily robbed me of speech. I stood dumb, mesmerised by that golden stare. At last I was able to stammer, 'Of course I didn't know. Dee, I'm so sorry. Melissa never mentioned it—we never thought to ask how he died. We assumed—a coronary or something. His age, you know.'

'In fact, he was a very fit and agile man. The fact remains, he fell over the edge and died of multiple injuries.'

'Dee, how ghastly!' All these years later, I could still feel the pain of my own father's death. How much greater the loss must have been felt in such circumstances, so futile and unnecessary. Poor Dee.

And Melissa? Was it this that had caused the state of mind that had so worried Gran?

Dee laid a large calm hand on my arm. She had recovered more quickly than I.

'Forgive me, this must have been a shock to you, but I thought you should be warned—we wouldn't want anything like that to happen again, would we? Try to put it out of your mind, dear, and have a nice day.' She paused, looking down at the tips of her immaculate white shoes. 'I really am surprised that Melissa never told you, though. But then, she loved my father very much.'

'Did she?'

'Oh, yes. He was a very lovely person, you know,' she said, softly. 'Well, it's all in the past now. Nothing will come of raking over old bones.'

Coming from the rather precise, even pedantic Dee, this struck me as a curiously inept turn of phrase.

I stopped to pick up a fallen hibiscus blossom, still perfect, its creamy petals flushed with rose, and with a laugh, tucked it into my hair.

The sun was hot, but prevented from being unpleasantly so by the ever-moving clouds. Already, the unhurried tempo of the island was communicating itself to me, and I dawdled along, enchanted, lingering in the glancing light reflected on the tiers of the scented terraces that made up the extensive gardens, criss-crossed by a maze of little paths and rocky steps. A small detour beckoned me; rounding a corner, I came with a small shock of delight on the source of the water I had heard.

The waterfall poured down over the black basalt rocks that formed the bluff behind the house, its first fierce impetus broken by a series of graduated drops, so that it finally fell quite gently into a wide pool at its foot.

I walked slowly along the pool's edge. Here the water was deep, but so clear you could see the flat rocks that formed its base. Further along, it became more shallow, to fall gently over the rocks and continue its downward descent. I wondered about swimming here. It seemed a natural swimming pool, sheltered and safe—lucky indeed on this island of no beaches, where the rocks rose directly and dangerously from the sea.

Kneeling, looking at the reflection of sky and cloud and my own wavering face in the water, I scooped a handful of the small pebbles that shone like opals beneath the surface of the water, admiring the iridescence of them on my palm.

Scrambling to my feet, I retraced my steps back on to the main path and began the steep, winding climb. Once or twice I paused, glancing up at the red-roofed chalet when it appeared, hoping I wouldn't have to pass it, that Ben Battista wouldn't be there if I did. I was out of luck, on both counts. Just as it came into sight once more round the last bend where the path forked, the left prong swinging away to a fair-sized building I took to be the studio, he came out of the door. Almost as if he'd been lying in wait to intercept me.

'Hi, there!' he called from three feet above me. 'I see you're finding your way around. Is it living up to expectations?'

'It's great—super! Is that the studio along there?'

'Yes. Melissa's already there, working,' Ben informed me.

'I know, she must have been up for hours.'

He jumped down on to the path in front of me, landing with knees bent, cat-footed. His blond hair was the colour of barley in the sun. His lean body was tough and fit, his short-sleeved T-shirt revealed powerful muscles. His smile was dangerously loaded with charm. 'I wouldn't advise going there—if anyone disturbs *me* when *I'm* working, I moan like the clappers. Why don't you come in and have a cup of coffee with me instead?'

'Thanks, but I've just had breakfast. And I do want to have a word with Melissa.'

'Not a good idea! She went haring up to the studio first thing, as though the devil was behind her—that, or inspiration. And as you may or may not have gathered by now,' he said, carefully choosing his words, 'that last hasn't been happening too often lately.'

My vague premonitions about Melissa all at once crystallised into solid, tangible fright. The things she'd begun to say last night became apparent. Work had always been the most important thing in Melissa's life. It had totally absorbed her, above friends, above family. If that hadn't been going well recently, it might explain practically everything.

I stood thinking about it, until I caught his quizzical glance on me, and had the uncomfortable certainty he'd engineered my response. 'Thanks for telling me. I won't keep her more than a minute in that case.'

'She won't thank you for disturbing her at all.'

He stood immovable in my path, with no obvious intention of shifting, waiting for me to comply, so sure that I would, so confident in his own attraction which, let's face it, was pretty potent. I felt my colour rise. 'Excuse me,' I insisted.

He grinned and made no move and the situation threatened to become ridiculous. I could hardly force my way past him. Swiftly, I calculated there was bound to be another way round to the studio.

'Maybe I'll leave it for now, then—though forgive me for thinking that you do take rather a lot on yourself, regarding Melissa.'

It was a face-saving accusation on my part, with a basis of truth, and for a moment I thought I had pierced his self-confidence.

An unguarded expression passed across his face, but he merely said, 'I've a good reason to—which I might tell you about some time, but at the moment it's you I feel responsible for. It occurred to me that with both Melissa and Dee working, you might be at a loose end on your first day here.'

Was that the impression I'd given—mooning around looking for someone to entertain me, when I was perfectly happy on my own?

'That's nice, but I don't have to be carried around, you know—I've plenty to occupy me.'

Ben nodded, thoughtfully. 'I have to go and see a friend this morning, a Dr Matios who runs a small children's clinic near here, just over the hill. I'll take you up there and introduce you to Jorges, if you wish. I think you'll like him.' He added, 'We missed the chance of getting to know each other yesterday, maybe we could remedy that, too.'

Oh, very cool, that 'we'! Still, I decided to go along with him. He had been pretty ghastly last night, but if he felt he owed me something, and he was determined on doing penance…

'All right, thanks. I'll come with you. I don't mind living dangerously.'

He grinned. 'This time we shall be walking, not driving.'

That made it safer? I thought, following him, as over his shoulder he told me he first had to collect some things—and in case Melissa should wonder where I was, he would leave her a note. She usually called on her way down to the house, and would know where to look. I made no comment, as he stepped aside to hold open the door.

'Make yourself welcome. Hardly five star, but it suffices.'

'You should see some of the grotty dumps I've been in and around these last few years,' I told him, noticing the clean, almost monastic plainness of the chalet.

It hardly seemed big enough to contain him. He had to stoop under the lintel as he went into the next room, which as far as I could see was the kitchen. The room where I stood was little bigger. White walls, two straight wooden chairs, a narrow hard-looking bed, several well-filled bookshelves. A table on which stood a typewriter and sheaves of papers completed the furnishings.

'If you want a more comfortable seat, you'll find the bed's the best bet,' he told me, coming back with two steaming mugs and handing me one. 'This coffee's not as good as it would have been earlier, but if you can take it, it'll save perking fresh.'

'I always use instant, anyway. This is fine.' I sipped, staying where I was on one of the chairs, preferring it's austerity to the disadvantage of having to look up at him while I spoke. As he wrote the note and tucked it under a plant-pot on the windowsill, I said, looking at the work on the table, 'Why Madeira? Why choose to stay here?'

'Bury myself, you mean? The classic answer—why not? I've loved the island ever since I came here for holidays with Felipe's family when I was a small boy. I came back a couple of years ago for peace and quiet and because treatment was available at the clinic—and there's night life in Funchal, and an excellent air service to most parts of the world if I want a taste of the *dolce vita*—which I frequently do.'

I told him I'd heard he put in a lot of time with the children at the clinic, too.

'Oh, Melissa!' he said with a soft laugh. 'She thinks it takes me from my work. But I have to be up there quite a bit, so I hang around and try to be useful—though Jorges—Dr Matios—has things pretty well organised in that direction. Those kids are his life.'

'What sort of clinic is it?'

'Orthopaedic, with many of the children long-stay patients. Jorges can't take as many as he'd like to; those who are there are deprived in one way or another.' He reached out an arm and took a cardboard tube from a shelf, the sort used to hold rolled-up drawings, adding negligently, 'My own treatment from him's nearly finished. Only physiotherapy once or twice a week now.'

A Handful of Shadows

I mentioned the helter-skelter cautiously, remembering my previous brush-off. He grinned. 'One of the more mobile children became over enthusiastic and, jumping to stop him, I twisted myself. Set me back a few weeks, that's all.'

And that, I knew, was as far as I would get.

He suggested we might take the path rising behind the *cabine*, which followed the course of the *levada*, rather than the road, though it wouldn't be easy walking, he warned.

'What's the *levada*?' I asked, and he explained as we set off that it was one of the hundreds of irrigation channels constructed to direct water from the high mountain springs—an effective way of supplying water and preventing erosion of the precious soil from the precipitous slopes into the sea.

But it was erratic as a source of domestic water supply, being channelled in turn to various districts. I understood the significance of Marian Lopes's remark now, and was glad I'd grabbed the opportunity of a bath.

After that, there was little chance to talk: the stony zigzag path was too narrow to walk side by side, too steep to leave breath for speech. Like some oriental wife, I plodded obediently in his wake, along a path which presently entered the thick dense forest that overlooked the house.

A cloud passed across the sun as we went in, and no light filtered through to relieve an atmosphere unpleasantly humid and close. Damp ferns, head-high, brushed dankly against me, and tendrils of creeper snagged my blouse.

'Somebody ought to have taken a machete to this lot long since,' I gasped, panting behind Ben up the seemingly vertical path.

He laughed and slackened speed. 'You mustn't be disrespectful to our famous laurel woods. Botanically speaking, they're unique—several rare orchids are supposed to grow here. Apart from the fact that everything else grows twice its normal size.'

None of this was reassuring. I felt as though I'd escaped when we finally broke through into brilliant sunlight and found we were on the summit, where by common consent we flung ourselves down on a patch of the sparse dry grass.

Once I'd regained my steadiness, I felt I could have stayed up there all day, on top of the world. It was all right, I found, if you didn't try to look straight down. You could see the sea from here, beyond lesser hills, far away. A little to the left I could hear, but not see, the waterfall where it fell over the lip of the cliff. Perhaps those were the red roofs of Funchal in the distance. Higher, behind us, rose the sharp, jagged peaks, cloud-ringed and sapphire blue, of the Pico do Aeriero. Six thousand feet up, where Oliver Newman had met his end.

I turned away from them, sick with vertigo at the mere thought, and met Ben's deep, curiously-coloured eyes watching me with embarrassing closeness.

'We must press on,' he said in a little while, not making a move. 'I've work to do this afternoon.'

'Your next book? I'm afraid I haven't read your others yet, but I'm going to.'

'You don't have to apologise, for Pete's sake! No one's going to pretend they're great literature. I'm not the intellectual type.'

'Oh, but surely...' A suspicion that he was being facetious crossed my mind, but his expression was quite serious.

'No. I've found my own level. Better that, I reckon, than make a botch of something beyond reach. As long as I can believe what I'm doing has some value, and still feel it stretches me, what more can I ask?'

He spoke with all the assurance and confidence of a man fulfilled in his work. Then what was it that gave his face in repose that strangely regretful look? Did he still hanker after the thrills and excitement of the racing career that had been cut short? What *was* it that had happened at the time of his accident? No use, memory slid away like water through my fingers.

'What about you, Christy?' His voice broke into my thoughts. 'What are your hopes and ambitions?'

'Me? Oh, I'm not the ambitious sort.'

'What do you intend to do now you've got your degree, then?'

'I don't know.' In a burst of candour, I admitted, 'You were right yesterday. I did come here to cry on Melissa's shoulder, in a way. I don't want to be a drag. Trouble is, though, I don't know what to do, and as long as ever I remember, she was always able to straighten me out.'

'Yes. She's surprisingly good at that sort of thing. Me, for instance—I don't think I'd ever have carried on writing if it hadn't been for her. I was a fairly hard case of self-pity when I arrived here.'

'You?'

'Uh-huh. I'd never have done that first book without her encouragement.'

'Isn't that underestimating yourself? I'd have thought you couldn't write a book without having it in you.'

'Ah, but it's getting it out! She made me see I wasn't defeated. You know how she is.'

We exchanged understanding glances, united in appreciating this lovely thing about her. She had always been able to imbue other people with her own special kind of joy, her zest for living. And looking at him, I saw that the irony habitual to him had vanished, dissolved into that same look I'd seen on his face the night before, when he had held her hands between his own and kissed her.

I broke off a piece of grass and chewed it fiercely. I said, 'I've only just heard this morning how Oliver Newman died.'

His expression didn't alter, but I sensed an immediate gathering of wariness in him. 'Are you saying you didn't know before?'

I shook my head. 'Melissa never told you?' he asked, as disbelieving as Dee had been.

'No.'

He seemed to find this fairly incredible, and took time to think it over. 'Maybe that's understandable. It's not a subject she'd want to talk about,' he said finally, shrugging. 'She was very shocked and upset, naturally.'

'She still is, isn't she? Even though she's been married to Felipe for over a year!'

'That's understandable, too—it's a very nasty way for anyone to die, to fall like that and be killed.'

I said, 'Tell me, *did* Oliver fall—or was it suicide?'

'The verdict was accidental death, Christy,' Ben insisted. A hardness had crept back into his voice. 'And believe me, it's better left that way. Oliver Newman is dead, and how he died is immaterial. It doesn't matter, now.'

But it did matter, if the repercussions were still echoing, capable of affecting others. There were shadows obscuring the truth like the shadows on the mountain sides, ghosts like those wraiths of cloud, which must be laid. 'What sort of man was he?' I persisted. 'Was he the sort to take his own life?'

'Oliver Newman,' Ben said, 'was the sort to do anything he chose.'

He stood up in one smooth, co-ordinated movement, held out his hand and pulled me to my feet, and I knew as I felt the unyielding grasp and saw the opaque look of his eyes, that as far as he was concerned, the subject was closed. I had effectively ended our moment of communication.

CHAPTER II

The clinic turned out to be a much more imposing building than the Quinta Miranda, but colour-washed a bright, pastel pink and built on a tiny plateau, surrounded by a high wall and evergreens.

Hot and thirsty after the steep climb, I was inclined to dally in the shade cast by eucalyptus gums along the gently ascending drive—nowhere was *flat* on this island—listening to Ben's explanation of how the clinic had originally been built during the last century as a nursing home for tuberculosis sufferers. It had gone through many changes before Dr Matios had bought it and made it into the clinic it was now.

Simultaneously with our arrival at the front door, a dusty and battered car roared up the drive behind us, and with a painful screech of brakes stopped just short of where we stood. The door was flung open and a dark, youngish man, his hair flopping over his eyes, leapt out. 'Ha!' he cried, flinging an accusing hand towards Ben. 'Here at last I find you! How do I miss you, I ask myself when I drive, not ten minutes since, to your house and back?'

'Because we took the direct route, Jorges my friend,' Ben replied.

'You *climb*, over the hill? I am not pleased at that,' the doctor said severely, beginning to wag a finger at him. 'I am come down for my drawing, to save you the trouble to walk, and there you are not! Well—OK, OK, maybe you are not so stupid, but then...'

'We're being shockingly ill-mannered,' Ben intervened hastily. 'Let me introduce Miss Christy Durrant. Christy, this is my good friend and sparring partner, Dr Jorges Matios.'

Instantly, the other man turned his full attention on me, abandoning his argument with Ben. 'I have heard you were coming, the daughter of the delightful Senhora Battista. And very nice also, I think.' He took my hand in a warm and rather moist clasp, flashing a gold-stopped smile at me. 'I am so glad to acquaint myself with you, Mees Durrant, and I would like to offer you some tea, only—' he ran his hand through his hair— 'I think perhaps there is none...Ha, I have it! Some of our wonderful Madeira wine! The English like tea, but they also like our wines, do they not?'

The Madeira my father had liked had been very sweet, and I would have preferred something more thirst-quenching.

'Thank you, Dr Matios, that would be nice.' I couldn't bring myself to dampen his buoyant enthusiasm by refusing.

'Ah, *bom*. *Bom*. Then immediately, in two shakes, you shall have some. Come, come in—is time before the children finish their rest.'

The hall, light and large and airy, with a wide staircase leading from it, and next to that the open door of a lift, was evidently used by the children. There were low chairs and tables, several bookshelves, some bright pictures and children's drawings pinned to the walls. A small flower-filled shrine stood in the angle of the stairs.

Dr Matios waved us to take seats and went out for the drinks, but I went first to look at a picture in an alcove. 'Yes,' Ben said, 'it's one of Melissa's.'

Even without the tiny bee which signified her name in the corner, I would have recognised it, by the subtle smoky colours she used, the feeling of movement, but as I looked at it more closely, I became aware of a difference.

Her pictures were always so simple it was easy to class them as facile work, done without effort. I knew the hours and weeks of patient toil that went into abstracting everything that hindered the purity of line and form. And that was where the difference lay in this one—it had prettiness rather than beauty; it was overworked, and lacked the simple strength and power of her other pictures.

I told myself that she had deliberately painted it this way for the children, and yet I was unaccountably disturbed by an impression that somehow her work had deteriorated.

The chilled golden wine which the doctor brought back within a few minutes and poured into a strange selection of odd glasses was unexpectedly dry and refreshing.

This was not the sweet malmsey which the English knew as the only 'Madeira', he explained with a twinkle, but *sercial*, a distinctive aperitif, no? It was necessary to understand there were several wines grown here— though the best person to inform me on that score would undoubtedly be Senhor Duente. Mees Durrant had not yet met him? He was a wine exporter...amongst other things, the doctor added drily.

The hall was cool and pleasant, the wine slightly soporific, and we leaned back, relaxing in low chairs arranged to overlook the shade of the gardens.

All at once, the quietness of the moment was shattered as two small boys erupted into it. The first was a lumbering lad of about ten, followed by a virtual tornado of a child, his small face contorted with fury under a large black cowboy hat pulled well down over his eyes. He wore a heavy calliper on his leg but it seemed to impede his progress not at all. Nothing had impaired his vocal cords, either. He caught up with the bigger, older boy, hurled himself on him, screaming and scrabbling like a little wildcat.

'Manuel!'

The command from the doctor had little noticeable effect. The small child clung to the other, blubbering boy like a monkey, butting his head against him, fighting tooth and nail.

Before Dr Matios had time to put down his glass and reach the two of them, a heavy, swarthy girl in a white cap and apron had appeared and separated them. His wails increasing, the bigger child disappeared, and then the nurse proceeded to shake the smaller one, haranguing him in Portuguese all the while and ending her tirade with a furious swipe to the side of the head.

He dodged it, and she looked up, her mouth falling ludicrously open as she saw that the hall was not empty as she had evidently expected, that Jorges Matios was standing over her, his face dark as he directed an avalanche of words at her.

As soon as he drew breath, the nurse scuttled off the way she had come, and the doctor re-joined us at the other end of the hall, Manuel held firmly by the hand. Manuel was silent, but not at all subdued, I thought, looking at the smouldering black eyes in the sallow face.

'So,' the doctor said to us, breathing heavily. 'She goes, that one, at last! I have had too much of her. She is, what you say, a bully, and I will not have that with my children, Mees Durrant, not even with this devil-child Manuel.'

'You've dismissed her?' Ben asked.

'I have given her the push—yes,' Jorges answered engagingly, with a return of his fourteen-carat smile. 'And now, what are we to do with you, Manuel, my friend?' He spoke quietly for several minutes in his own language to the boy, whose unrepentant expression didn't change, and then, sighing a little, sent him away. 'He is at war with the whole world, poor Manuel,' he said, as we watched the boy stomp away with mutiny in his hunched shoulders, his hat resting on his ears. 'He is much disturbed; his mother has died recently, and now there is only a grandmother. His leg will soon improve, but alas, I fear for him—here.' Dr Matios laid his hand on his heart.

It was an oddly touching gesture, all the more so after that display of anger. I studied him covertly, a man sensitive and emotional, but by no means weak. Yet capable of temper and impulsive actions, perhaps even ruthlessness in getting what he wanted.

'And now, Mees Durrant,' he said briskly as a bell rang somewhere in the background, 'the children will be having lunch soon. You would like to look round my little kingdom, no?'

He hauled himself to his feet, and I followed suit with alacrity. 'Please, I'd love to see what you do here.'

'Ben?'

'No, you go on, and I'll help mind the shop.'

I followed the direction of his glance. A few of the children were already coming into the hall, one in a wheelchair from the lift, accompanied by a girl in a white overall, some walking with the aid of sticks or callipers, all of them laughing and chattering as uninhibitedly as children anywhere. They gave me curious, friendly looks as I passed with the doctor, and several of them went across at once to Ben. With them went the white-overalled girl, very pretty with thick black curly hair, who blushed like a peony when Ben spoke to her.

Ben noticed my backward glance as I went out of the room with the doctor. 'Give these children an inch and they take a *milha*,' he grinned, as they swarmed around him.

*

'Well, how goes the verdict?'

Ben was waiting for us after our tour of the building, in the small room which served as Jorges's study.

'Oh, fantastic!'

'Fantastic?' he echoed sardonically.

'Well, what I mean is, warm and friendly. Not a bit like a hospital—the children actually seem to *like* being here!'

I felt warmed myself by the radiance of Jorges's smile as he listened to this praise, although it hadn't been intended as flattery—I'd been genuinely impressed. During the tour, I'd met the rest of his patients, those who were confined to bed in the wards which opened on to a wide veranda running the length of the building at the back, and anyone must have been blind not to draw the obvious conclusion that everything was disposed as far as possible to create a happy family environment. Those who could get about had comfortable bedrooms, shared with two or three others, scattered with their small personal possessions and with ample evidence of their interests and hobbies. They were light bright rooms with small religious pictures on the walls.

I noticed that there was every encouragement for the children to chat with the staff, who were led by a large, efficient sister called Rosa, and to try and help with the chores—despite the fact that it might have been quicker for the nurses to have done everything for them. The staff were run off their feet, and would surely be yet busier after the dismissal of that other nurse. I asked Jorges.

He spread his hands, rolling his eyes in a very Latin way. 'I fear so, yes. We have much difficulty, you see,' and he went on to explain that a shortage of staff was one of his main problems. He did not have the means to pay large wages, and most young women—those of any training, I must understand—would not work in this isolated spot without such incentive.

'Alas, all the spare money I have must go on the improvement of my little clinic. I borrow the money, Mees Durrant, and until all is paid back, I must tread with care, otherwise, I shall be in the soup! Is hard, no? But if something means very much one does not count the cost, I think. My life is not luxurious, everything I own is in this house, these children. But is the dream of my life come true,' he added simply.

A small boy on an exercise machine designed as far as possible to look like a Formula One racing car, was trundling himself up and down the corridor where we stood, making the appropriate noises. Jorges, bending down to steer the child on a straight course past us, whispered something which made the child shout with laughter.

'Yes, I can see what you mean,' I said gently. I liked this mercurial man, found his use of English slang endearing, and admired his seriousness of purpose.

He watched until the child manoeuvred himself safely round the comer. Then he turned back and continued speaking. 'Perhaps I have been too lucky, so far. Not everyone has so much good fortune.'

I had moved to the window, and he came to stand by me, and pointed out the roofs of the Quinta Miranda below. Plainly visible from here, above the encompassing laurel wood, was the way the boundary walls of the clinic formed the apex of a rough triangle, driving a wedge downwards between Melissa's land and the Duente house. This last was a modem, split-level dwelling, an arrangement of white, interlocking cubes perched on the rocky hillside.

'How good that you are here!' Jorges said. 'For yourself, of course. But as a doctor, I think it will be good for your stepmother. As a friend, I should like to see her happy once more.'

So my concern for Melissa was not groundless. I sensed an ally in this man, and his words encouraged me to believe he would be prepared to discuss things openly. On the spur of the moment, I asked, 'Did you know Melissa's husband—Oliver, I mean —well?'

He made no reply, his eyes following a car that was beginning to snake down the drive of the Duente house. He leaned forward, opening the window wider as if he suddenly found it difficult to breathe, and took out a handkerchief to mop the sweat that beaded his brow. Without turning round, he said, 'Oliver was once my friend. It was he who lent me the money to buy this place.'

'Oh,' I said, and added conventionally, 'his death must have saddened you.'

'Saddened me? Oh yes. Is always sad to lose a friend' he answered, almost to himself, still gazing out of the window. 'More perhaps when that friend has deceived you.'

'Oh, dear, I'm sorry... '

He waved a hand. 'No, no. Is I who say too much.' The car disappeared from view and Jorges, breathing heavily, turned away from the window. I caught sight of his face and knew a moment of fear. The sweat stood again on his forehead, his face was grey. In the space of a few minutes, he looked infinitely older. Was he ill?

He saw me start forward and pulled himself together, almost literally, it seemed. 'Shall we go on, Mees Durrant?' I looked at him uncertainly, but in a few minutes he was nearly his cheerful self again, leading the way to the office where Ben waited.

Ben was unrolling the drawing he had brought with him, spreading it out on a low table. 'Come and hold this corner, there's a good girl,' he said to me, disposing ashtrays and a paperweight to hold down the other three corners.

I knelt between the two men, looking at the drawing with interest. It was a rough sketch Jorges had made for a proposed extension wing to the clinic, and they began to discuss the pencilled notes and alterations Ben was suggesting. It appeared to be a fairly ambitious plan, and apparently the same thought was belatedly occurring to Jorges. As they talked, his face grew longer. 'Why do we speak of this?' he cried eventually. 'We shall need *money*! As well to wish for the moon!'

'Castles in the air again, Jorges?' said a cool, light voice.

We had all been so absorbed for the last half-hour that none of us had heard the car arrive, nor seen anyone come in. I knelt back and saw the shadow across a beam of sunlight, a slender sandaled foot near me. Looking up, I saw the elegant owner of the sandal, and at the same time the men scrambled to their feet.

Introductions were made. Caterina Duente smiled neutrally and didn't offer to shake hands—but her arms were full of parcels and flowers.

'For your patients, Jorges,' she announced casually, showering him with expensive boxes of chocolates and bird-of-paradise flowers, exotically unreal-looking, waxy purple and orange. 'I had a winning streak at the Casino last night. Poor Felipe, I believe, was not so lucky.' She made it clearer. 'Your stepmother's husband,' she said, and for the first time allowed herself to meet my eyes. There was an amused appraisal in them.

'You go to the Casino, Caterina? Alone?' Above the armful of flowers thrust on him, Jorges's liquid eyes were shocked, reproachful.

She shrugged. 'What of it? You must learn to move with the times, *querido*. They are not so old-fashioned in England,' she said, sliding a glance at me, 'or they were not when I was at school there. My mother was English, Miss Durrant.'

Which accounted for her excellent command of the language, but I hoped not for her offhand manners.

She added, 'I don't suppose the children will have your scruples, Jorges, when they are eating the candy.'

'Caterina, Caterina, how many times do I tell you? You must not waste money on things of this nature. There are better ways of helping my children. Your two hands would be more welcome than—all this.' There was still a trace of reproof in his voice, but he had softened. His eyes, when they rested on her, his whole manner, gave him away. Jorges Matios was in love, and no prizes for guessing with whom.

She lifted her elegant shoulders, seeming not to see the hurt in his eyes, nor to hear the suggestion of pleading in his voice, and spoke to Ben. 'But I am not cut out to help in those ways, am I, *querido*?'

He answered her with a quizzical lift to his eyebrows. 'You can't know. You've never tried.'

'Nor do I mean to, my friend. It's not a gift given to everyone. But I see you don't agree. Miss Durrant.'

'I don't know, I've never tried, either. But Dr Matios,' I said to Jorges, 'it looks as though I might have quite a bit of time on my hands while I'm here. Since you do need help—d'you think—is it possible I might be of some use?'

Too late, I was acutely aware of three pairs of eyes upon me. Caterina's speculative, Jorges's startled, and Ben—the unexpectedly furious expression on his face made me blink. I ploughed on. 'In a totally unprofessional capacity, of course, but I suppose there must be things I can do for the children — help them dress, or have their meals. I don't mind wiping noses, something like that...' My voice trailed off uncertainly.

'My dear and charming Mees Durrant! You would give up your holiday, for this?' Jorges's astonishment had quickly given way to a gratified pleasure.

'Miss Durrant isn't going to be here long enough to give up anything,' Ben said.

'Oh, but I am, if a couple of months is enough.' My chin went up a fraction. 'And anyway, I wouldn't be giving it up entirely, just a few hours here and there to lend a hand, Dr Matios—but please say, if you'd rather not.'

More than anything, I didn't want him to feel obliged to use me if it embarrassed him to do so, if he felt I was an amateur do-gooder who might be more of a hindrance than a help.

Jorges, however, was looking delighted with the idea. 'But this will be absolutely nice! I was not wrong—you are a very lovely girl indeed, Mees Durrant...Christee.'

Caterina's eyebrows lifted superciliously, although she smiled as she picked up her soft suede handbag, ready to go.

A clock struck somewhere. Jorges looked at his watch and immediately became fidgety. I turned to him to say goodbye and we discussed briefly how I would arrange my hours at the clinic. He wouldn't let me feel pinned down. I was to come only when and if it should be convenient for me. He shook my hand warmly with both of his when we left.

Outside the house, Caterina opened the door of her car. 'There's room on the back seat, Miss Durrant, and Ben—you can have the front seat if you move those parcels.'

'Thanks,' I said, 'but I think if you don't mind I'll go back as I came, on foot.'

My eyes met Caterina's, and neither of us pretended it wasn't a challenge. In fact, my calf muscles were already protesting at the unaccustomed climbing, and I was well aware they would feel worse on the way down, but it was infinitely better than being ordered into the car by this tiresome girl.

But she wasn't giving up easily, either. 'Ben, walking will take time from your afternoon's work, will it not? I will have you back in a few minutes.' She put her hand possessively on his arm.

'Do go ahead,' I told him. 'I can find my way back without any difficulty.'

His frown was fastened on me. 'Thank you, Caterina, but not this time...I'm well organised as far as my work's concerned.'

'Oh, but—' she began. She was not very clever, I thought. Didn't she realise he wouldn't take kindly to being anyone's property? A faint trace of colour appeared in her olive cheeks. She eyed me narrowly for a moment, then with ill grace accepted his decision. Fluttering her eyelashes, she murmured, 'I'll see you tonight, then, *querido*.'

He answered her with a disconcertingly intimate smile, and she swung her legs into the low seat of her car, let in the clutch and made a stylish exit down the drive.

Caterina, Melissa. Which? Or did he like several strings to his bow? I followed him slowly back through that awful wood, conscious of the unspoken disapproval of *me* in every stride he took.

*

I said goodbye hurriedly when we reached his *cabine*, but he stopped me with a hand tight on my arm. 'Before you go—' he began, and any hope that his annoyance with me had faded disappeared.

'Yes?'

'Since you seem bent on ignoring my advice not to stay here overlong, I must ask you one thing.'

'Must?'

He wasn't the only one who was angry, but he chose to ignore my tone. His grip on my arm was painful. 'You want to help Melissa, right? Then don't probe old wounds—unless, of course, you're prepared to do something about them when they're re-opened.'

His warning fell like little chips of ice, all the more sharp and hurting after our previous friendly interlude. 'I don't follow. Are you suggesting,' I said coldly, 'that I would poke my nose into Melissa's affairs?'

'Not knowingly.'

'Then you are saying there's no way she can be helped?'

'I'm saying just that. Not by you, at any rate...nor me.'

'I don't believe that. I'll *never* believe it.'

He released me, stuck his hands in his pockets and stared at my face. At last he said softly, 'Christy, Christy! You come here with stars in your eyes and flowers in your hair—no, leave it, I like it—'

I felt a fool as I put up a hand to retrieve the forgotten, fading hibiscus blossom and crushed it furiously as I recalled Caterina Duente's barely concealed amusement.

'—and keep the stars, too, as long as you can. But remember, things aren't as simple as you seem to think. You can't set everything to rights with a laugh and a kind word.'

'Why not?' I demanded. 'Why not try, at least?'

'You're very young,' he said, 'but nice. Don't change.'

It was the kind of remark to which there is never any answer.

'There aren't any half measures about you, are there, Christy? I suspect that when you love, you love whole-heartedly, and sometimes it overwhelms your common sense. But can I ask you at least to make me this promise?'

'If it's the same as the last request, no.'

'Just give me your word to come to me with anything you don't understand before you act on it. You'll always find me here.'

His slow, deepening smile was for me, now. And I felt afraid. He was the one person who would be pleased if I packed my bags and left Madeira this instant, the one of whom every nerve and instinct told me to beware. Yet I had a trapped feeling, amounting to panic, that if I needed to confide in anyone, he would have the power to draw me to him. I shivered because there was a quirk of pleasure in the thought.

I had an urgent compulsion to disperse the intensity of feeling that twanged between us like a taut bowstring, and I gave a light half-promise.

'But would it be such a good idea? I'd be afraid of disturbing you in the middle of some purple prose!'

'Ouch! But not to worry. If you hear the record player going, you'll know I'm working, and the louder it is, the harder I'll be at it. There's nothing like music for generating a head of steam.' He reached out and caught a tendril of my hair, letting it corkscrew round his finger. 'What a girl you seem to be for getting involved! I hope you're not going to regret your impulsive offer to Jorges.'

Deny it as I might, he could be uncomfortably near the mark, I thought, as I plunged down the path to the Quinta, as if he divined the self-doubts already beginning to chase through my mind. Had I, regrettably, offered to help at the clinic not through altruistic motives but because Caterina Duente had needled me into it?

Indignantly, I dismissed the idea—the gesture might have looked phony, but it was nothing of the sort. What was wrong with offering to share my bit of spare time and surplus energy with someone who needed it? Besides, I thought, it might be fun.

All the same, passing the pool by the waterfall, I tossed a pebble into the shining water for luck.

*

I was relieved to find that lunch at the Quinta was a hit and miss affair, for whoever happened to be there at the time. Dee was taking lunch at the Duente house, and Melissa was still in the studio. She had given orders, Marian said, pursing her lips, that she was never to be disturbed there. Marian would bring me a light snack out on to the terrace at the front of the house. Mindful of the slight clash of wills with Marian that morning, I didn't demur, and within a few minutes of sitting down there, she had brought out a tempting tray.

As she laid it down, I told her, in an attempt at conversation, that I had visited the clinic that morning, and the other's pale eyes gave me a sharp look. 'He's a good man, the doctor,' was all she said. 'Very well thought of on the island.'

'I'm sure he is,' I agreed warmly. Then curiously, I asked, 'Do you like living here, Marian?'

'Well enough.'

'You've never thought of going back to England?'

'I've no ties there. My boys were born here and they've a good family in my husband's relatives. Portuguese families are very close, they love children and they have a sense of obligation.' She smoothed down her nylon overall. 'I don't think I've forgotten anything you'll want, but I'll be in the kitchen if you need me.'

She gave a slight nod, and her stocky figure disappeared round the corner of the terrace. Not exactly forthcoming.

After I'd eaten, I wrote a letter to Gran, a difficult letter, without saying too much about Melissa, and then I went into the sitting-room in search of Ben's books. I decided to take all three of them and read them in chronological order. Closing the heavy glass doors of the big bookcase, I looked round for a comfortable place to sit. I decided immediately that the terrace was a much better idea.

I'd only glimpsed this room the night before; now it struck me as more dreary than the dining-room. There was the same weighty, dark furniture, a large brown couch whose leather was cracking, armchairs in a rubbed dark blue and maroon plush, a Turkey square on the polished floor and curtains of wine-coloured brocade. It might have been a comfortably handsome room in its way, only...It was a while before I realised what was wrong.

There were spaces on the walls where lately pictures had hung. Every other surface had been swept clear. The walls of the room, the whole house, I now realised, its tables and shelves where works of art, or at least pretty and interesting trivia might have been expected to be displayed, were bare and unadorned.

There were no table lamps, flowers, or even plants, no pictures of any description. Very few people chose surroundings so completely devoid of ornamentation. It seemed odd, to say the least, that a house which had belonged to two such artistically-minded people as Melissa and Oliver Newton should be so devoid of charm, of anything that might have given it colour, or another dimension. It was more than odd, it was strangely creepy.

Perhaps it was Felipe, Melissa's present husband, who was responsible. My curiosity about him was growing.

I held the book on my lap as dusk became darkness, and I sat for a while with my eyes closed, thinking about what I'd just read.

I'd thoroughly enjoyed the book, *At Top Speed*. It was in the unputdownable class, with a rattling pace and a witty, concise style. The exciting, nail-biting, jet-set background of top-class motor racing was there too, and something of that compulsion that motivates a man to choose a lifestyle that means constant gambling with death. But of the essential character of the man who wrote it—nothing.

I stood up and went indoors, through the unlighted sitting-room behind, where a frenzy of yapping startled the life out of me.

Someone said, 'Here, you bad animal, it's only Christy—give him a pat, then he'll shut up.'

'Melissa! What on earth are you doing here, sitting without any light?'

I reached out a tentative hand to Heathcliff who leaped back neurotically, but at least left my fingers intact. Switching on the light, I saw Melissa huddled in a chair. She blinked as the low watt bulb bathed the ugly room in a kind, disguising glow that made the garden beyond recede into blackness. 'I didn't know you were out on the terrace either, my love.'

I saw she hadn't yet bothered to change from the washed-out smock she always worked in. The wide, loose neckline left her slender throat bare and somehow vulnerable, like a child's. With her bare feet and without her make-up, she might well have been a child sitting there. Closer to, she looked worn and spent.

I knew I mustn't let her see how much her appearance shocked me. I launched into a bright account of what I'd been doing, and if I overdid the enthusiasm, she didn't appear to notice, merely remarking she was glad I'd enjoyed my first day here. I was about to tell her of my suggestion to help at the clinic, when I realised how inanely I was chattering. 'I'm sorry—here am I rattling on, and you must be dead tired. You've been slaving away since first thing.'

She gave a peculiar little laugh. 'Work should make me feel like this! But yes—' and a spark of animation lit her frozen features—'I have made some preliminary sketches. I'd like you to give me a sitting tomorrow morning, if that's all right with you. It's early days, of course, but I think there's a chance it might be going to work out.'

'That's great.'

'But if not, it might at least get me going again.'

Here it was, the lead-in I wanted. Ignoring Ben's warning, I went across the room to sit on the floor beside her, hugging my knees. 'Tell me to keep my nose out of things if I'm interfering—but what's worrying you, Melissa? Something is, for sure. What is it, that exhibition in San Francisco?'

'There isn't going to be an exhibition.'

'Oh no! Why not?'

'Because you can't have an exhibition without pictures, and you can't paint pictures if you haven't got what it takes any more. On the other hand, maybe I never had—what it takes, I mean. Maybe it was only Oliver's doing that my work sold at all.'

I didn't for a moment believe this. I didn't believe that Melissa believed it either. And the thought flashed through my mind that wasn't all this a bit theatrical, a bit overdone? I said lightly, 'Come on, you know that isn't true! But it all sounds highly dramatic. So what's gone wrong, Stepmama?'

The old jokey name evoked no answering smile. 'If I knew that,' she came back with a touch of sharpness, 'I wouldn't be worrying about it, would I?'

I frowned. 'I don't see that necessarily follows. If you can't work properly, there must be a reason for it, mustn't there? Like something on your mind.'

'Don't start psychoanalysing me, love. Any minute now, you'll be telling me to pull myself together.'

This unfairness was altogether so unlike her that I felt a sharp sense of hurt astonishment. I think she realised this, and said more moderately, 'I've always been able to keep my private and professional lives in separate compartments, you know that. Never in my life has anything ever stopped me working. Personal problems have nothing whatever to do with this.'

She was deluding herself. The very vehemence with which she spoke gave her away; there was a touch of hysteria underlying what she said. She picked Heathcliff up and began nervously to separate the strands of hair on his head.

'No, this is something quite different.' She slid me a look out of the corner of her eye, hesitated before going on. 'What would you say if I told you that there is something, someone, maybe, deliberately trying to stop me...something—evil?'

Cold fingers seemed to walk my spine. This was worse than I'd imagined. I said quickly, 'I'd wonder whether you weren't being-well, over-imaginative.'

It was the wrong line to have taken, and I knew immediately I had lost whatever confidence I might have gained from her.

'Don't be like that, Christy. Don't be like everyone else. Not you.' She sounded desperately disappointed, bitter and accusing.

You couldn't blame her, I told myself, struggling to believe it, biting my lips to stop the protest that sprang to them. Maybe I hadn't come up to the mark, but no one could say I hadn't tried. We were dangerously on the edge of a row, and rows were something Melissa and I just didn't have.

We sat on in silence for a few minutes longer, then she stood up, Heathcliff tucked under one arm. 'You're right, of course. Silly, isn't it? Too stupid for words.' She looked lost and disorientated. 'I was just on my way to change. Supper's around eight.' She stretched out her free hand and took mine, and her strong, thin fingers felt like a little claw. 'Please, I'm sorry. I hate to see that look on your face. I'm not being cagey,' she said with magnificent dissimulation, 'it's only that I don't want you mixed up in what's going on around here.'

She seemed to have forgotten that she had previously said the very thing to spark off the kindling, and unaware that she was now adding fuel to the fire.

'I am mixed up in it, if you are,' I said, stubborn with fear for her. 'It's something to do with Oliver, isn't it?'

What little colour there had been in her face fled from it. 'Leave it,' she said in a dragging sort of voice. 'No, Christy, I mean just that—leave it alone. I expect things will work out in the end. They usually do, don't they?'

She threw an arm round my shoulder and gave me a hug, warm and loving again, but with a kind of desperation in it. She went upstairs, her footsteps light as a whisper on the treads.

And I couldn't get rid of this feeling I had, that she was running into some kind of disaster and that I, who loved her, was powerless to prevent it.

When I went into my room a few minutes later, the wind was billowing out the curtains, and on the wooden floor by the window was Dave's photograph, smashed into a thousand pieces. I was sure I'd left it on the bedside table at the other side of the room. I concluded that Josefina or Marian must have been up here to dust, and unthinkingly put the photo on the chest by the window where the wind had caught it.

Gingerly, I picked it up. Dave's face stared up at me, splintered into unrecognisability, and I felt sad and rather frightened, as though it were symbolic of a whole lot of things. As though, in the same way that his photo was altered by the shattered glass, I too was in danger of being changed.

Already, I was beginning to feel deeply involved and committed to things I sensed might change me, and I wasn't sure if I welcomed or was afraid of the feeling.

*

So this was Felipe. A slow-moving man, heavily built, with a long, handsome, olive-skinned face. He was maybe approaching forty, his hair just beginning to recede at the temples. Agreeable and attentive in a serious, correct way, he was talking in careful English about the island, passing me vegetables, filling my glass, informing me that the distinctive, heavy scent I'd noticed was frangipani.

'I thought that only grew in the tropics!'

Felipe waved a soft, well-kept hand on which flashed a small diamond. 'Yes, but anything grows here. It is to do with our fertile soil and our moist, temperate climate. You will see many types of subjects from all over the world growing quite happily in their season—camellias, flame trees, orchids, as well as every kind of fruit you can imagine. Most of them were brought in as an experiment, like my bananas, but very few things failed. So you see, I have special reason to be grateful.'

He obviously had a deep pride in his country, and showed his pleasure in my appreciation. His urbane presence, immaculately tailored in a grey, lightweight suit with a whiter than white silk shirt, brought welcome normality to a day I felt had been quite fraught enough with tensions of one sort or another.

Candles had been lit, and the glow had a softening effect on the room. It was a pleasant and leisurely meal we had together. Melissa seemed to have recovered from her depression, or at least to have put it behind her, though she was quiet and preoccupied, letting the others take the lead in the conversation.

'You'll be able to see the flame trees,' Dee took up where Felipe had left off, 'but what a pity you've missed the flowering of the jacarandas. They're quite spectacular when they're in bloom.'

'As you will see, if you are looking for an ardent supporter of our island, or someone to tell you its history, look no further than Dee,' Felipe intervened with a slight smile. 'She knows even more about it than I, who was born here.'

She glanced quickly at him, a flush warming her pale skin, but it was impossible to suspect Felipe of anything so unseemly as sarcasm. Looking from one to the other, I wondered how he really reacted to having the daughter of his wife's former husband living permanently in the house with them, a situation which surely had the makings of discord in it—he and Melissa not long married, still in love—or at any rate, not obviously out of it, as I had begun to fear.

'Perhaps that's because I'm so fond of it all,' Dee murmured in her understated way. 'Of the island, and of this house—I have been ever since my parents bought it as a holiday home when I was a child.' The amber eyes glowed for a moment, before she went on, quickly, covering any embarrassment her statement might have caused, 'As for history, there isn't much anyway. The island wasn't discovered and settled on until the fifteenth century.'

She smiled at me and asked if I should like to see the island, and offered to take me to Funchal the next day when she went shopping. I was sorry to have to refuse. I loved new towns—towns new to me—but I explained about my commitments—sitting for Melissa, helping at the clinic.

'You've lost no time,' she remarked, 'but how nice that you won't be alone when Melissa is busy.'

'Oh yes,' Melissa said, beginning to peel an orange. 'I'd forgotten about it. Caterina told me.'

'Caterina?' Dee asked sharply.

'Mm, she'd been up to the clinic, then she came over to the studio to deliver a note to me on the way back, round about lunchtime.'

'A note?' Felipe repeated slowly.

There could have been something comic in this echoing of everything she said, but I saw the unwilling conspiratorial look that passed between Dee and Felipe, and I sensed undercurrents that were not in the least funny.

'Oh, not one of *those* notes,' Melissa said, opening her blue eyes very wide. 'Just something quite trivial and unimportant, from her father.' Her hands were tense round the orange.

Dee ate a piece of cheese, then said mildly, 'I wonder why Senhor Duente didn't give me the note to deliver?'

I wondered, too, why Caterina hadn't asked me to do so, but not for long. She wouldn't have asked me to pass the salt if she could help it. All the same, she hadn't struck me as the sort to go out of her way unnecessarily, especially since it seemed apparent there was no love lost between her and Melissa.

Unless…a possible explanation of Melissa's behaviour before dinner occurred to me. Could Caterina have been anxious to deliver the note in order to have the satisfaction of imparting information about Felipe's activities the previous night? Had Melissa really believed in that mythical business appointment last night? Was Felipe an habitual gambler? He wasn't a man to give much of himself away, I thought, watching him getting on impassively with his dinner. As if aware of my scrutiny, he looked up at that moment, smiled, laid down his napkin and began to steer the conversation into safer waters.

*

We were finishing the meal when Melissa asked Dee if she would pick up some things for her the next day when she was in Funchal, adding that she would give her a list of the items she wanted.

'Surely. Anyone else need anything?'

'If it's not too much trouble,' I said, 'I seem to have had an accident with a photo-frame of mine. I think the wind's blown it over and it's broken the frame as well as the glass—though I could have sworn I left it on the bedside table, well out of reach of the wind.'

I was quite unprepared for the effect my casual words had. Dee stared at me in an appalled sort of way. Very deliberately, Felipe finished off the wine remaining in his glass, and Melissa, playing with her fruit knife, dropped it clumsily, her gold seal bracelet clattering against her plate.

'Oh, Christy! Why you?' she breathed.

'It doesn't matter,' I said hurriedly. 'Not in the least. The photo itself wasn't damaged, and the frame was only a cheap thing. Probably Josefina moved it to the chest without thinking when she dusted. It could easily have blown off there.'

'It wasn't Josefina,' Melissa said, colourlessly.

'*Namorada*, I thought we had dropped all that nonsense.' Felipe put a soothing hand on her arm.

'It's happened before?' I asked.

'We seem to have in this house what has been called,' he said with an amused look at Dee, 'some kind of poltergeist.'

'Oh!' I said blankly. 'Is that why...?'

'That's right. That's the reason the house looks so bare,' Dee intervened to answer me. 'We have had a spate of unexplained breakages—almost amounting to destruction. So much that at last it seemed safer to lock away what has survived. It's all been—very disturbing.'

'It was merely a series of misfortunes,' Felipe said easily. 'You have said yourself, Melissa, that Josefina is what you call butter-fingered. She is afraid to admit what she has done for fear of losing her job here.'

'Misfortunes!' Melissa's face was the colour of the parchment linen mats on the table.

She looked piteously at Felipe, and he said, '*Sim. Com certeza*. Certainly they were!' He smiled and said, 'Supernatural causes? Pooh! That is mere hysteria.'

His glance included Dee, as well as myself, and she protested, 'Have I ever said it was anything supernatural? But Christy, wouldn't you say it's rather too much to blame on one poor girl?'

I hesitated. Felipe's interpretation seemed on the face of it to be the most obvious explanation—yet even the most butter-fingered person must have been monumentally careless to have broken so many things. On the other hand, to think otherwise indicated the most pointlessly vindictive exercise I had ever come across.

What could the person responsible hope to gain by it — save satisfying some personal spite or enmity? Against whom? All the occupants of the house or—only Melissa? At that nasty thought, I shivered. Her earlier assertion of something working against her seemed less fantastic. And an echo of Melissa's question kept reverberating through my mind. Why me?

Felipe was speaking to Melissa again. 'Calm yourself, *querida*,' he was saying, taking her hand, folding the fingers and kissing them gently. 'We shall gain nothing by picking this over yet again. There are more pleasant ways of spending an evening. Perhaps Christy would like to hear some of our island music?' He pushed his chair back, and with a wave of his hand dismissed the subject. 'The solution is not to leave anything lying about.'

Melissa said evenly, 'That's not a solution, it's only shelving the problem.' But she seemed to have gathered a sort of dignity around her, and if her voice shook a little, she poured coffee from the percolator on the sideboard with a hand that was steady enough.

For the next hour, Felipe played records of the *bailinho* folk dance, carefree and lilting, soft and sad, that was the heartbeat of the island. Melissa had put a match to the pine logs in the hearth for appearance's sake, and their scent was sharp and pungent on the air. Felipe sat back on the leather couch and Melissa curled on the floor beside him, her head resting against his knee, her eyes closed.

A Handful of Shadows

No one spoke except when Dee, sitting under the low-lit central lamp, stitching at a piece of petit-point embroidery, broke in to explain the Moorish origins and traditions reflected in the dances: the rhythms representing the treading of grapes, the jogging of men carrying heavy baskets, the slow, restricted tread of the slaves brought to Madeira by the early settlers.

It was a peaceful domestic scene, but there was no feeling of peace within that room. The pine logs crackled blue and green, and goblin shadows leaped in the corners and on to the ceiling. Melissa's hands, clasped round her knee, showed her knuckles white, and Felipe smoked small, strong-smelling cigars incessantly; in the flickering light, his face had lost its soft melancholy and was all planes and surfaces, like the portrait of some Portuguese grandee.

Only Dee seemed outwardly calm and possessed, but once or twice when she looked up, I saw the lamplight set a flame leaping in her eyes and guessed that despite her calm, she was disturbed and anxious.

When the music finished, Melissa took the coffee tray, saying she would go straight up to bed. Felipe soon followed, but Dee and I sat on, talking in a desultory manner until at last she said quietly, 'I'd like to talk to you, Christy, properly, but not here.' She stood up, folding her work tidily, looking round her with barely concealed distaste. 'This room depresses me utterly…when I think of how it used to be—what it still could be. It's not the lack of pictures and so on, it ought to have been re-done years ago, but then, the expense, you see…Let's go up to my room, shall we?'

It was funny how people you knew to be absolutely loaded were mean about little things—to have had the whole house redecorated would have been peanuts to a man like Oliver Newman. It was surprising, too, that Melissa hadn't done anything about it herself—unless she'd been too discouraged by what had been happening.

I followed Dee up the stairs to a large room in the wing of the house. She unlocked the door and pressed the light switch, and the scene blossomed into life before my startled eyes. A white and green room, cool and refreshing as the heart of a lettuce. White furniture, white walls glowing like alabaster in the radiance of the lamplight, thick soft white rugs scattered on the polished floor, deep armchairs, one in emerald, one in ivy-patterned chintz, floor-length apple green silk curtains. Mirror-faced cupboards reflected the crystal on the dressing-table and made three images of Dee as she walked to one chair and offered me the other.

'Dee, this is fabulous!'

She glowed with pleasure. 'Do you like it? I'm so glad, I thought you might. I did it out myself.'

'Truly? You have a real flair.'

'I sometimes used to think I might like to be an interior designer,' she admitted with a regretful sigh. 'But other things intervened. My mother, you see, was very delicate, and I nursed her until she died five years ago.'

'Five years—but surely, you were still—?' I broke off, trying to cover my embarrassment by touching with gentle finger a green ground-glass apple balanced on a polished ivory stand.

'My father gave that apple to me when I was a very small girl. I've built the whole room around it, to remind me of those happy times.' A small curious smile played round the comers of her mouth. 'No, I was over thirty when Mother died, Christy, too old to start without training or capital. The only money I had was a small income left me by my grandfather, just sufficient to keep me independent, and I decided not to risk losing it.'

If Dee's mother had died five years ago, I calculated swiftly, at the same time wondering why Oliver Newman couldn't have provided his daughter with the money she needed, that meant he must have married Melissa very soon afterwards.

The train of my thoughts may have been apparent, for Dee said, 'They married pretty quickly, Melissa and my father.'

'And you didn't resent it?'

'Oh no,' she said quickly. 'Well, perhaps a little—I wouldn't have been human if I hadn't, would I? But that was before I met Melissa. Afterwards, I was glad to see him happy. Some men need a woman beside them. Especially my father—he had so much affection to give.'

I was filled with admiration for her, and sensed that quiet strength of which Melissa had spoken. How many women could have accepted a situation like that in such a well-adjusted way? Especially since Dee had loved her father with an apparent blindness to the faults others saw in him.

She moved serenely across to the other side of the room. Picking up a coloured, framed snapshot from a circular white table, she brought it over to me. 'This was my father, taken a short while before his death. He was a fine man, wasn't he?'

I had never seen a photograph of Oliver Newman, and it was a shock to see this one now. My image of Oliver Newman had been of someone grey-haired, perhaps a bit portly, a tycoon-figure of sorts. Certainly not this dark, smiling man, posed in self-awareness of his own good looks and virility, on the deck of a boat which had 'Melissa' lettered on the bows.

Clad only in brief white shorts, he looked fairly devastating in a well-barbered, gleaming 1930s' film-star way. And young enough to be Dee's brother, never mind her father.

She said gently, 'He wasn't much over twenty when I was born. He and my mother made a runaway match. It was quite romantic, in all the best traditions, the handsome, penniless young man and the rich heiress—she was from one of the oldest Boston families, you know. My grandfather didn't approve. I guess he would have cut her off with a dime if her fortune hadn't been tied up for her so that he couldn't!'

Looking again at the photograph, I found no difficulty in sympathising with Grandfather. If ever a man looked an opportunist, Oliver Newman did. And no man could have appeared less like a suicide. With relief, I realised that to believe his death was anything but a tragic accident was ludicrous.

Dee's story was intriguing. So that was where Oliver's wealth had originated—from Dee's mother. What, I wondered cynically, had been in it for him when he married Melissa?

Dee took the photograph from me gently and put it back exactly where it had come from, adjusting a small green opaline vase another quarter of an inch to correspond, smoothing a hand over the white silk bedspread as she passed. Now that the initial impact of the room had worn off, it struck me how unlike it was to anything I would have expected…one would have imagined any room belonging to Dee as neat, comfortable and unobtrusive, a bit like Dee herself. Anything but this luxurious, even indulgent room. The fact of it made Dee seem a little less perfect, but at the same time a little more human.

'No poltergeist here then?' I asked as she came back to sit near me.

'Oh yes. I'm afraid I didn't escape. A small picture was smashed, but after that I kept my door locked. You see, I don't believe, either, no matter what Felipe would have you think, that these happenings have been caused by anything but a human agency—though that makes them even more horrible and puzzling, especially since, apart from that picture of mine, the malice has all been directed at Melissa. Until…'

'Until now,' I finished. I had no intention of allowing it to upset me, but still, I had to push down the feeling of unease. How insidious it was, this fear, this creeping suspicion that someone close could be wearing two faces.

'Has Melissa told you about the letters?' Dee asked suddenly.

'What letters?'

'She says she's been receiving anonymous letters—three, so far.'

The small shiver of tension that had passed round the room at dinner, when Melissa had spoken of the note Caterina had delivered, seemed to repeat itself, adding to the inexplicable apprehension growing in me. '*Says* she has?' I repeated.

'Ye-es.'

'Dee, are you trying to say that Melissa is *lying* about them? Why? What possible reason could she have for doing so?'

Dee was looking at me strangely, her luminous eyes sad. 'I hardly know how to say this, Christy, but she seems to have some sort of—well, I can only call it persecution mania. I have tried to get her to see a doctor, you know, or an analyst, on account of how her mother died...'

'No!' I almost shouted it. Melissa was volatile, soon up and down again, but never would she, as her mother had done, take her own life, never!

At the same time, the small, cold voice of reason told me that it could, just could, be possible. Melissa, for all I loved her, for all the joy of being with her, was not a very stable character, and the shock of Oliver's death, which was in some way blocking her ability to work...this in turn leading to her inventing an excuse for it, that she was being hounded, chased...the need to convince others of it with tangible proof...dear heaven!

Dee heaved a deep sigh. 'It doesn't bear thinking about—but I can't tell you how glad I am that you've come here, my dear. For one thing, you're a sensible girl, and I've never been able to confide my fears about Melissa to anyone before, not even to Felipe...especially not to Felipe. He won't listen to me. He prefers to shut his eyes and believe nothing's happening, I'm afraid.'

I wondered just how much of this was coloured by the quality of Dee's personal relationship with him... but maybe he always did take the least troublesome way out. Gambling, after all, was only another facet of this, a belief in the false promises of an easy way to instant success.

'Poor Felipe,' she went on, 'he inherited a rundown business from his father, which needs a business head to put it right.' Was there just a shade of contempt in her voice as she added, 'All the money in the world won't help without that.'

Melissa's money? I thought rather cynically.

'But as for Melissa, she's all bottled up inside herself. I've been so afraid—' She broke off, biting her lip. 'We mustn't talk like that, not even think it. She's terribly fond of you, your being here will surely help. She's already begun to take the first steps, with your portrait. If we don't probe too deeply, she'll soon forget all this other business.'

She was so genuinely distressed about Melissa's predicament, her sensible attitude was an obvious one to follow. I was thankful for the fact that she was here, supporting Melissa. But I was still anxious. To believe what Dee had suggested, I also had to believe that Melissa was a consummate actress, hiding secrets behind a cloak of duplicity, she who had always been an open book. I wasn't ready for that, yet.

Nor was I ready for sleep, my mind was too full of the day's happenings. After leaving Dee, I slipped a sweater round my shoulders and took the path that led to the pool at the foot of the waterfall. It was a night of bright, white stars with no moon, and the pool was still and black. The great wooded cliff rose above me. In the eerie starlight everything seemed enhanced, sharpened, gigantic and distorted, unreal as a Disneyland grotto, and I myself dwarfed into insignificance. The sense of unreality crept into my thoughts, making the things happening here seem even more fantastic, yet more unbelievable.

There must be a simple, logical explanation! But none came as I sat on my mossy stone, tossing pebbles into the water in tune with my unease, making wide, ever-increasing ripples.

To the left on the hillside, a light burned in the chalet. I had the strongest impression that he, Ben Battista, held the key to the dark undercurrents present in Melissa's life, that he could tell me what they were if he wanted to, if he weren't so keen to dissociate himself. Should I try once more to persuade him, in view of what I'd learned this evening?

Careful! Hadn't there been too swift a reversal in his attitude, after I'd made it plain by my decision to help at the clinic that I'd no intention of leaving? Could be, for reasons of his own, he was wanting to keep tabs on me, side-track me if I came too near the truth. Even as I hesitated, I caught the faint drift of music—Stravinsky, wasn't it? Played loud enough to be heard down here meant he must be working at full pressure. I began to go back to the house, relieved that the decision had been taken out of my hands.

I had taken barely half a dozen steps before voices reached me, Melissa's and—Ben's, '...mean to say you haven't told him yet?' he was saying, forcefully.

'I will, Ben. I promise I will.' She was pleading, evasive.

I kept on walking towards them, but they neither saw nor heard me, and his next words glued my feet to the spot. 'We can't keep it from him. He is your husband, and he has a right to know.' He had hold of her arm, and he was being far from gentle with her now.

'Give me a little while longer...'

'How much longer do you *need*? It's been nearly a year already. Look, Melissa, I'm giving you an ultimatum. Either you tell him, or I will. I mean that. Make up your mind, you or me, which of us is it to be?'

'Let go of my arm, Ben! Sometimes you frighten me...'

'Ah, Melissa!'

I waited to hear and see no more. Softly, I retreated to the pool's edge, until, eventually, straining my ears, I heard their footsteps die away.

*

The clear island air made me feel alive and invigorated, and during the next few days I walked and took roll after roll of colour film which I probably wouldn't be able to afford to have developed. I sunbathed, and polished off the other two Ben McLeod books.

I sat for Melissa and managed several hours each day at the clinic, becoming familiar with every bend in the sinewy road that led there, heavily tree-shaded and offering glimpses below of secret, lush little valleys dripping vegetation, folded between the hollows of great craggy peaks. I knew I would never willingly take the zigzag path corkscrewing through the wood, however much of a short cut it was.

I was glad to find that Jorges did me the honour of expecting me to work as hard as the rest of his staff, calling on me to help out with everything from feeding small patients, to assisting Constanca, the physiotherapist, during exercise periods. But mostly my job was to help provide the mothering, playing games with the children, singing and teaching them nursery rhymes, trying to make up the loving which they missed from not being with their own mothers, and which Jorges considered so important. It didn't matter if I spoke or sang to them in English, a cuddle and a kiss were the same in any language.

All the staff showed me friendliness, from Rosa, the formidable sister-in-charge, downwards. It was like being included in a big, overgrown family where everyone pitched in to get a job finished. Watching the devotion of Jorges and his staff, I not only envied them their dedication, I was bowled over by their stamina. Goodness knows, I was no slouch, but I had all I could do to keep up with them.

Felipe took me down one afternoon to see his banana plantation, where I watched the great green hands of bananas being packed for despatch in the air-conditioned holds of banana boats. He apologised profusely for the rundown appearance of the place, the ramshackle packing sheds.

'Very shortly, however, I believe I may expect to see some change,' he said, blinking lazily in the sun, but with a secret, contained excitement about him. He kept what it was to himself, however, handing me with his usual exquisite politeness into his car.

On the way back, we passed Ben's car going in the other direction, its hood down. Caterina in the passenger seat, wind-blown and laughing.

Ben came the following afternoon to stand by me while I and two of the junior nurses, Maria and Luisa, gave an eye to the recreation of some of the more mobile children on the swings and the slide, whose steps were a disguised form of exercise in learning to walk. As I carefully lifted Inez, a little girl who wore a spinal brace, into a specially designed box swing, he asked, leaning against the next one, bracing his feet against the ground, 'Getting the hang of things?'

'It's not difficult— I'm only a general dogsbody, after all.'

'Exhausting?'

One of the boys shrieked with excitement as he swooshed down the slide into Luisa's strong, steadying arms. I laughed. 'Not so's you'd notice. I'm loving it.'

'And blooming with it. I can see you're making the most of your holiday.' Stressing the last word, he squeezed my arm. It was a warning, and my nerves jumped.

'Yes, I am. I expect to have learned a lot by the end of a couple of months.'

I let him make what he wanted of that, daring him to challenge my right to stay as long as I wished, but this time he wasn't having any. He gave me a half-salute and walked off with his loose-limbed, easy stride. Constanca, hovering, met him in the doorway. Chance often seemed to put her in his way. He stopped to talk to her and she blushed and fluttered, as they all did. Even Rosa, who was stout and brawny.

Watching the two of them, my memory stirred. Another girl, another time, a scandal connecting Ben Battista with her. Try as I would I couldn't recall more. He was still talking to Constanca, laughing into her pretty, upturned face. When he went indoors, she turned, smiling, set her pert cap more firmly on her curls and swung confidently away.

*

Melissa was waiting for me when I arrived from the clinic a few days later. 'I'm glad you're down early—have you had lunch? Oh, good. Let's cut the sitting and go on a spree in Funchal. Poor thing, you deserve a break, and I need one, too. Put your best bib on, and we'll go shopping, then I'll give you tea at Reid's.'

There was that controlled excitement about her again, that vibrating vitality, as though she were on tiptoe. I needed no persuasion, I very much wanted to visit Funchal, and it was more than a bit boring, truth to tell, sitting for Melissa.

She hadn't even begun to paint yet, and was still covering sheet after sheet of paper with sketches, most of which she'd discarded, until I began to lose my stiffness and self-consciousness. 'Move about, loosen up,' she ordered. 'Laugh, chatter, cry if you want—this mustn't become static, whatever happens, because that's a thing you simply never are.'

Once she began to paint, she assured me, she would work quickly, getting the idea on canvas. Meantime, I had to curb my natural energy and impatience, and sat or stood in a dozen different positions, my hair up, my hair down, full face, three-quarter face, profile, even with my back to her. At the same time, at the other end of the studio, a huge abstract was taking shape which she was working on in the intervals of drawing me.

I knew she liked her mind to be busy on one while her hands were occupied with the other. Oddly enough, it seemed to work. She was at it in the studio from dawn to dusk, and looked excited and happy. Not a trace of the wan, trouble-burdened woman I had previously seen and worried about. I was amazed.

I washed quickly, changed from jeans into a cool cotton frock and put a comb through my hair. I was running downstairs within ten minutes, passing the telephone as it began to ring. Automatically, I reached out to answer it. The deep, guttural voice at the other end asked for Melissa, who had just come in and was standing by the door, raising enquiring eyebrows. 'Who is that, please?' I asked. 'Oh, Senhor Duente.'

A Handful of Shadows

Before I could hand it over, Melissa was shaking her head violently. With a look of stubborn refusal, she turned on her heel and swung out of the door.

'I'm afraid she's not available at the moment. May I take a message? This is Christy Durrant, her stepdaughter.'

There was a heavy pause at the other end before Duente's thickly accented reply came back. 'Since she refuses to speak to me, you may ask her why she does not answer my letters, that is all. Goodbye, Miss Durrant.'

How much of a person's character is revealed by his voice? I only knew an instant and intense antipathy towards the owner of that one, a frightening feeling of power and coercion which had come across the wires, and the certainty that the burden of his message, the significance of which I had somehow not grasped, held a threat.

Melissa was already sitting in the driver's seat of the small green Ford which bore ample evidence on its left side of frequent contact with the rock face when its driver had taken a hairpin bend too sharply. Her hands were tense on the wheel.

'What did Duente want?'

I repeated what he had said, and without comment or explanation, she started up the car with a jerk that nearly threw me through the windscreen.

She drove as fast and as badly as ever. I'd ridden at some peril to my life with carefree students in beat-up old bangers and never turned a hair. I'd also travelled the same route in reverse, with Ben Battista at the wheel, scared only of the road, not the driver's ability. Now it was both.

I managed not to show my jitters for most of the way into Funchal, whose red roofs appeared now and then below us. When we were coming into the town, and the traffic was increasing, she shook herself out of her withdrawn silence, taking one hand off the wheel to point out a cruise ship lying in the bay. I swallowed, and concentrated hard on what I could see of the town and its approaches.

Funchal appeared to have escaped the worst sort of brash holiday development; I guessed the island, with its lack of sandy beaches, wouldn't easily lend itself to that.

I rolled down the window. It was much hotter here than in the mountains, but the cobbled, tree-shaded streets with their wide, mosaic pavements promised a cool oasis from the heat, though bustling with shoppers and invaded by passengers from the cruise ship. Not a moment too soon for me, Melissa parked the car near the town centre, turning off the ignition with a triumphant gesture. 'There, that was all right, wasn't it? And goodness knows how long since I last drove. Felipe doesn't care for me to, on these roads.'

And Felipe might have reason, I thought, baulking at the prospect of the journey back.

American cruise passengers, cameras clicking, were burdened with souvenirs, basket ware, bottles of wine and fruit. Carnations and beaky bird-of-paradise flowers filled their arms. Their cabins back on board would overflow with the scent and colour of the blossoms which spilled from the baskets of the flower-women by the cathedral, a fleeting reminder of the island of flowers.

'You are going to see absolutely everything!' Melissa said, with a determinedly bright smile I found almost heart-breaking.

Obviously she was not going to let that telephone call spoil my day, but, knowing her and loving her as I did, I could see that the fear and tension in her were almost ready to spill over.

CHAPTER III

For several hours Melissa and I wandered through the narrow alleys and the wide main thoroughfares of Funchal. We shopped relentlessly for embroidery and wickerwork for Gran, and Melissa pounced with delight on several yards of brilliant red and gold damask for me to wear for the portrait.

'There's no need to make it up—we can drape it around you with the same effect. It's perfect, exactly what I had in mind,' she declared. 'Now, tea!'

Reid's hotel was full of the rich from everywhere, I realised as we negotiated its English Edwardian splendours. Intimidating, when you were hot and grubby, hung about with bulky parcels—and possibly the only person under thirty in the place. But here on the covered tea terrace it was nice painted basket chairs, chequered tablecloths and a view of the blue bay over the waving tops of the feathery palms.

The first person I saw was Caterina Duente, and it took less than a split second to recognise the back of the person she was with. Ben. They seemed to be having a disagreement. I could see her scowl from a distance of thirty or forty feet, and the hunched set of his shoulders as he leaned forward, talking.

And while I wouldn't go as far as to say it pleased me to see them quarrelling, I was human enough to prefer that sight to the several times I'd glimpsed them together as I sat for Melissa, an unwilling spectator through her window to their intimate, friendly entrances and exits from Ben's chalet.

Melissa had seen them, too, and immediately went to them, threading her way between the tables. Neither saw us straight away. Caterina was doing the talking now, shaking her head and not troubling to lower her voice. 'My father would never speak to me of it,' she was insisting angrily. 'But if there was such a deal, what does it matter now? That man is dead, thank goodness—and I will promise nothing!' She was oblivious of our approach.

'Hello, Caterina. Hello, Ben,' Melissa said.

Ben looked up quickly, the frown still on his face, but instantly it was wiped of everything but pleasure when he saw who it was. He sprang up at once.

'Won't you join us?' he asked, looking more delighted at the prospect than Caterina. He welcomed Melissa with the special attention reserved for her—at least in public. And then he turned to me, his smile lingering when our eyes met, his hand brushing mine, not entirely by accident. It was humiliating to feel such pleasure.

After the fuss of settling in and having our tea brought over, he leaned back in the deep wicker chair. 'How's the portrait, Melissa? Not demanding too much, I hope, to stop you coming to Jorges's firework party for the children.'

'I'll be there—we all will.' Melissa smiled.

'How about adding your persuasions to mine? I was just trying to get Caterina to induce her father to come along as well, wasn't I, Caterina?' Her lifted eyebrows indicated surprise at hearing this, but she didn't deny it.

The statement was a tentative question, exploring how much we'd heard of their conversation, that much I realised. His eyes searched our faces. I tried to look impassive and Melissa busied herself pouring China tea, handing me wafer-thin brown bread and butter. She, at least, gave no indication that Caterina's words had been audible to half the room.

Caterina had been too absorbed in herself to notice then, and didn't seem to care now. She sat sideways to the table, leaning against the wrought-iron rail of the terrace. 'Papa won't come, he never does anything for pleasure—unless it's the pleasure of making money,' she said rudely.

She really was the most boring girl I'd met in a long time.

*

By the time we arrived back at the Quinta Miranda, the island's capricious *capacete*—a thick, damp mist—had come down, but the coolness was balm after the heat of Funchal. I splashed myself with cold water, chose a fresh dress and left my room.

I was still bothered by that telephone call Melissa received from Duente and didn't feel like letting the matter go entirely. It had shattered Melissa, and I had a strong suspicion, reinforced by my own impression of his voice on the telephone, that she was in some way afraid of him. I wanted to know more about him, and there was one person who could tell me—Dee, who worked for him and saw him practically every day. Dee could always be trusted to see things from a balanced viewpoint.

I sought her out, but she wasn't in her lovely green and white room, so I slipped on my jacket and went out into the garden, making my way towards her favourite spot at the top of the waterfall, where she was often to be found at this time of day.

It was a grey evening, the cloud vapour obscuring the late sun. I could hear Melissa's voice calling to Heathcliff as I passed the pool, looking faintly ghostly in the mist, the pink chalice flowers of the water lilies at the far end folded like hands in prayer.

'Is the pool dangerous?' I had once asked Dee. 'Is that why no one uses it for swimming?'

'No, no, it's perfectly safe,' she had answered quickly. 'What makes you ask that?'

'It's occurred to me once or twice that it's a natural swimming pool, and with the shortage of such on the island...'

'No one ever does use it—not since I was a child.' She had looked faintly affronted at the idea of anyone else doing so, before giving a small shrug and smiling. 'I don't know of anything against you doing so, if you wish.'

So far I hadn't take advantage of this, and at the moment it looked far from enticing. Soon it was out of sight as I climbed the stony path that was scarcely more than a scramble, twisting as it did around the wooded cliff, avoiding the shorter, precipitous route up through the woods.

'This is why I come up here, Christy,' Dee had told me, the first time I had come across her, sitting on a pile of large boulders that were balanced with such nonchalance near the edge of the water that they seemed about to tip over any minute. 'It was my mother's favourite view, too. She used to bring me up here most evenings before I went to bed. It's worth the climb, don't you think?'

Tonight, however, she wasn't here, and there was no Technicolor sunset out and away over Machico Bay, only the clammy mist obscuring shapes, and the muted roar of water.

The waterfall began here, a rushing stream emerging from the forest and cutting through high rocks, dank and mossy, to pour over the vertical cliff face. The stones where Dee usually sat were large and solid enough, though nearer the fall a small wooden railing had been set up, useless as a barrier, but enough to warn the unwary or the venturesome.

The sound I heard then, piercing the rush of water, was thin and high. A sharp little bark that faded to a tired whimper. I stood still, listening, and it was repeated. I looked around me, but could see nothing, and was answered by another faint bark. It was coming from below the waterfall's rim.

Steeling myself, I leaned over the crazy railing. I didn't dare to look for more than a fraction of a second, and the mist obscured the total view, but it was enough to show me the shining fall of water, the jagged teeth of the black rocks thrusting through the turbulence at the points where jutting escarpments stayed its downward flow. And on one tiny ledge, a dripping shape clung miserably—Heathcliff. I had to draw back instantly, closing my eyes against the sick, reeling sensation.

As I did so, I heard a footfall, scrunching over the scree on the hillside and relief swept over me. I called out to Dee. The footsteps halted, and I called again, but there was no answer. 'Dee? Is that you? I'm over here by the waterfall—I need help. Dee? Dee?'

I could hardly believe it when the footsteps, not Dee's quick decisive pace, but heavier, slower, moved away from me. I began to run in their direction, then stopped. This mist was deceptive—to blunder about in it foolhardy. The footsteps died away completely, and Heathcliff gave another hoarse, terrified whimper.

Away from the edge, the feeling of vertigo receded, and I forced myself to go and take another quick look. This time I was prepared, and directed my gaze not down, but sideways to the ledge where he stood shivering. I saw he'd been saved from slipping off by his collar being caught on a thin tree root or plant that grew from a crevice. It looked a desperately frail support, likely to give way any minute. There was clearly no time to go all the way back for help.

I strained my ears, listening hopefully for a return of that footfall. Whose? Who could have left me, ignoring my call for help? Not knowing that it wasn't me who was in danger? I could hear no returning footsteps, and my heart began to thump sickeningly against my ribs as I realised what I must do.

Another swift, stomach-lurching glance downwards showed me that the rocks between which the waterfall fell were wet and slippery with algae, but otherwise not difficult to climb down, and the spot where the little dog clung could not be more than several feet below the top. If I could reach him, I was sure he could scramble to safety himself. The difficulty lay in being able to control my own fear, the dizziness, that might overwhelm me and send me crashing down on to those rocks.

I sat down on the clammy grass, twisted round and lowered my leg over the edge. One step at a time; deep calming breaths. 'Be thankful for the mist that conceals the true extent of the fall beneath you. The climb itself is easy—easy ... ' I felt the rising wind, cold on my skin. I was level with the dog, and as I stretched out my hand to grasp his collar he bared his teeth in a snarl of fear.

I couldn't reach him from where I stood. I daren't, I mustn't lean too far. I closed my eyes in fright and frustration, and clung to a small tree-trunk that grew out at an angle from the rock face. It was then I heard footsteps. Heathcliff barked, I called again, and a voice answered me. 'Is that you, Christy?'

'Ben!' I gasped in relief. 'I'm down here!'

The mist was clearing. I could only look up, and cling to the tree trunk. But I could see a patch of blue sky, and Ben peering over the edge, and I saw how ludicrously near the top I was, though I might as well have been a hundred feet down. My first blind gathering of courage had completely deserted me.

'What the devil...?' he began.

'Heathcliff's caught on a branch or something down here. I can't reach him!' I was almost weeping with a mixture of fear and relief.

'Never mind that. You climb back up, then I'll go and get the dog. I've a longer reach than you.'

He had no idea how much the climb down those few feet had cost me, of my fear of heights, no notion that my limbs were trembling to such an extent I wasn't sure whether I could haul myself up without falling backwards. My hands felt nerveless, my body paralysed, but I could see that there was no room for two on those rocks. I could imagine no way he could get me up except by going to fetch a rope. I must get myself up. I must *not* think of falling. I hooked my arm more firmly round my small tree, and with its aid, and the sheer instinct for survival, scrambled somehow on to the next rock above me. A pause. And then the next. The next, and a pair of strong hands reached out to mine, pulling me ignominiously up the last few feet. I stumbled shakily from my knees, and for a single, blessed moment, I was held in the circle of strong arms, safe and sheltered. 'The dog...' I murmured.

'All right, I'll have him up in a jiffy.' He was gone, and I was alone, and my legs suddenly buckled under me. I collapsed on to the grass, and fear for him made the bile rise to my mouth as I heard the scrape of his feet descending.

And then he was beside me again, a small, shivering, dripping bundle in his arms. 'Are you all right?' he asked me.

I nodded. The mist had practically cleared, with its usual suddenness, and the evening sun going down in a glory of crimson was comfortingly warm on my icy body. He gave me a swift appraising glance, a smile touching the corners of his mouth. I must have looked perfectly normal for he simply nodded. 'You'll do,' he said, taking off his jacket and wrapping it around Heathcliff.

I followed his hurrying feet down the path. The swift scramble back down the hillside was maybe the best thing for me. By the time we reached the bottom, I was beginning to warm up, my legs had ceased to tremble. My hands had changed from icy cold to burning. I looked at them and saw that my left palm was scraped raw, my nails broken. What did it matter? I was alive, when I might have been a shattered heap on the rocks below.

When we reached the division of the path, Ben said, 'I don't think we should let Melissa see him like this.'

I agreed and went with Ben to his chalet, where we rubbed the little dog's coat dry. 'He'll be none the worse,' he said, pouring me a measure of brandy, and sliding it across the table. That and the brief moment of tenderness after I had climbed back over the edge, were the only indications he gave that he might have sensed my fear and tension.

'Heathcliff must be the luckiest animal alive—what are the chances against his being caught and saved like that?' I asked. 'And even so, it's a wonder he wasn't throttled.'

'He was supported by the ledge—and that tree root was stronger than it looked,' he answered shortly. 'It wouldn't have given way.'

'But you couldn't see that from the top—and it was lucky for me, too, that you came along when you did.' I wouldn't have given much for my chances, otherwise. In fact, his arrival had been almost uncannily well-timed. 'How did you happen to be up there?' I asked slowly.

'I was heading that way. Melissa was out looking for the dog—weren't you, too? I went up after you, because it's not a nice place to be alone in the mist.'

I shook my head. 'I didn't know Heathcliff was missing—and what would he have been doing up there anyway?'

'Chasing a rabbit?'

Heathcliff's rabbit-chasing days were long since over. Any spirit of adventure had deserted him long ago—he scarcely left Melissa's side nowadays. I looked at him, dozing off the after-effects of his adventure, and I said, 'Just after I found him, someone else came up there. I couldn't see who, and when I called for help, whoever it was went away.'

The glance he gave me was wary and watchful. 'Footsteps, Christy? I never met anyone. Sounds can be deceptive in the midst.'

'What other noises are there up there to confuse them with?'

He stood up, walking with his athletic economy of movement into the kitchen, carrying the damp towel and my empty glass. I had no idea whether he was trying to avoid a direct answer, or simply exasperated at my over-active imagination. I *had* heard footsteps moving towards me, then away again. A slower tread than either Ben's or Dee's. Slower, because that person had been treading deliberately softly.

When he came back, I said, watching him, 'Look at this,' and showed him Melissa's gleaming gold bracelet, heavy with the weight of the numerous seals suspended from it. 'I found it on the rocks near the dog.'

He looked at it, not attempting to touch it, his eyes narrowing as if making some quick calculation. 'She could have dropped this days ago. And if what you're leading up to is some nonsense about persecution complexes, forget it. I just don't want to know.'

The last of the sun filtered through his window in a haze of dazzling gold, and through it I saw him, handsome, controlled and aware. I couldn't begin to guess his reasons, the peculiar ambivalence of his attitude towards Melissa—if he were in love with her, how could he continue to abstract himself from her problem?

I saw him staring at me, and I had a crazy feeling that he was as aware as I was of the strong physical and emotional attraction that flared between us. I turned away from him. I just didn't understand anything.

'Whether you want to know or not, you'll admit that's what it was meant to look like?' I said. 'No one will seriously believe that Heathcliff went up there himself. He was *put* on that ledge, and whoever put him there would have found him, no doubt with witnesses—and found the bracelet, too. It was meant to look like another of Melissa's make-believe acts against herself.'

'In that case,' he said sardonically, neatly fielding the accusation and bringing the discussion to an end, 'you could foil the attempt by not mentioning where you found him. He seems to have survived the adventure pretty well, and he won't talk,' he said as Heathcliff yawned, got up and stretched, 'will you, old boy?'

*

Melissa was telephoning when I went to her room before our meal. I made to leave again, but she motioned me to stay, and I walked over to the dressing-table, sat on the stool and looked at the reflection of the room in the glass. Though it was shared with Felipe, it was very much Melissa's own; warm and alive and full of the careless clutter of her living.

In the centre of the bed, Heathcliff was curled like a Chelsea bun, complacent at all the fuss made over his safe return. Leaning over, I put out a finger and stroked his forehead. He opened one eye, but only made a token growl. I glanced at Melissa but she was a long way from me, absorbed with frowning concentration in what Felipe was saying on the phone. Taking the bracelet from my pocket, I laid it beside her watch and a couple of rings on the dressing-table. She wore the bracelet only in the evenings. If what I suspected was true, she wouldn't yet be expected to have missed it.

The receiver clicked back, and I swung round. Melissa was still holding on to the instrument. Her face wore a look of intense shock.

'Whatever's the matter?'

She sat quite still, fixedly staring at the tip of one gold-thonged sandal. Then she said, 'Here's a thing now! Felipe had a meeting fixed for today—someone going to join him, putting cash into the firm. Now it seems the other's backed out for some mysterious reason...unless,' she added suddenly, 'you count out Duente. Dear heaven, yes, I'm willing to bet all I have he's had a hand in this!' Her laugh was bitter. 'All I have! Christy, you and I have just got to make a success of your picture now—otherwise we shan't have a cent to live on.'

'Melissa! You're not dependent on *that*?'

'Angel, you are good for my ego, aren't you? Don't you realise what a Melissa Durrant's worth? Enough, at any rate, to keep the wolf from the door a while longer—long enough to prevent Felipe...'

She bit her lip and I said quickly, 'That wasn't what I meant. It's just that I thought with all the money Oliver left you...'

'What money? Most of what he left wasn't paid for, my love. Apart from this house, my legacy from dear Oliver wasn't worth a button.'

'But I've always thought...Dee told me her mother brought him a fortune.'

'It's not as difficult as you might think to go through even a million or two in a very short space of time, not when you're the sort of gambler Oliver was. Most people would have invested it and lived comfortably, but not Oliver. We'd been living off my money for ages when he died. This house was just about all he had left, which was why we came to live here—and that wasn't such a good idea, either, with the Casino handy. He'd win one night and lose it all the next.' She stooped, nervously pulled on her other sandal. 'Not that I care about money for its own sake, it's only that it makes me feel so helpless now, knowing I can do nothing to help Felipe out of this mess.'

My mind tracked to something she'd said earlier. 'You mean Felipe doesn't know—about your not having any money?'

'Felipe thinks, as everyone does, that Oliver left me plenty, and I haven't disillusioned him. When he's needed money for his business, I've been able to help him out so far by—realising assets. I thought once his business was back on its feet that would have been the end of it—and this time, anyway, he didn't ask me. I never anticipated not being able to go on earning.'

I was too stunned to say anything. She reached out and touched my cheek with cool fingertips. 'Don't look so unhappy. I love him, Christy. If I want him on those terms, that's my problem. You'll understand some day when you're in love yourself.'

I looked down at my hands, chilled by her bleak acceptance of the fact that Felipe would have no further use for her if he knew Oliver had left her penniless. Penniless? There were degrees of poverty. 'At any rate, there'll still be Jorges's mortgage repayments, won't there?' I reminded her. She looked blank and I prodded, 'The loan Oliver made Jorges for his clinic.'

'I know nothing about a loan, it's highly unlikely. Certainly no repayments have come from Jorges. Where'd you get that idea?'

'Maybe I misunderstood,' I murmured, knowing very well that I had not. The incident when Jorges had told me about it was still vivid in my mind. But Jorges not paying the money back? Cheating Melissa? I couldn't rid myself of the niggling reminder that he was undoubtedly a very worried man, and jumpy whenever the subject of his finances cropped up.

'I'm pretty sure—' I began, but she wasn't listening. She said suddenly, 'Be a love and tell Marian that Felipe and I won't be eating here tonight. I'll go back into Funchal and meet him and we'll eat out.'

She didn't actually say, 'Keep him from the Casino,' but her tone and her suddenly decisive manner said it for her.

'Of course I'll do what she wants,' Marian Lopes said stiffly when I passed on the message. Her whisk became still over the bowl of eggs. 'There's nothing wrong, is there?' she asked with uncharacteristic concern. Her neck had flushed a dull red.

'No, they've simply decided to dine out,' I added that Melissa had hoped it wouldn't put her out.

'It won't be the first time,' she replied ungraciously. 'Er—how's the little dog now? Where did you find him? We were looking all over.'

'Up on the hillside, and he's OK.'

'Are you sure?'

'Of course, why shouldn't he be?'

'Why, he's an old dog,' she said, and went back to whipping her eggs at a furious rate.

I went along to the sitting-room, and mixed Dee's favourite drink while I waited for her. She had been kept late working for Duente and hadn't long been in.

'My, am I ready for that!' she said when she joined me. 'I've had my nose to the grindstone since nine this morning. Where is everyone? That wasn't Melissa's car I heard just now?'

I nodded, and told her Melissa had decided to go into Funchal and have dinner with Felipe.

'What? Oh well, I guess he'll bring her back then, and have someone drive her car back here tomorrow—but it must have been something special to make her drive down there in the dark?' she ended on a question.

I twisted the stem of my glass round in my hand. 'I think she wants to take his mind off some disappointment he's had—some sort of merger he was negotiating, that hasn't come off. Melissa seems to think that Duente has stopped it.'

'That could be possible. He has a lot of influence—but isn't that just typical of Felipe?' she exclaimed. 'I'm afraid, you know, his trouble is this weakness he has for speculation—of any kind. Without foundation, since he's invariably the loser. Melissa does seem to have a genius for choosing such men. My father was a little the same way inclined,' she admitted ruefully, though this time with a small indulgent smile. Then she sighed. 'Well, Melissa's maybe a little foolish, too. I offered to buy this house from her some time since, at a good price, and I wouldn't have turned her out, but she wanted to keep it. Sentimentality, Christy! There aren't many of us who can afford it, however much money we have.'

The swift dusk had brought its usual chill. Dee closed the French doors to the terrace. 'Time to eat. We'd better go in. Marian doesn't like it if we keep her meals waiting. I hope you're hungry enough to polish off enough for four!'

'It's all right, she knows there are only the two of us.' Recalling our exchange in the kitchen, I said, 'What do you make of her?'

'Who, Marian?'

'There's something a bit off-putting about her, isn't there? Why do you think she stays here? It can't be much fun with her children in Funchal—and I have the impression she's not entirely devoted to Melissa.'

'Not entirely,' Dee answered with a dry little laugh. 'But she is to Felipe. She's been with him for years. I used to think he might marry her at one time. I guess Marian thought so, too, until Melissa came along.'

*

Young Manuel's leg was improving so rapidly he would soon be able to go home. He was, however, being uncooperative. He didn't want to go.

But this was understandable! Jorges exclaimed when Rosa tut-tutted and tried to persuade the little boy how wonderful it would be. He had been at the clinic for so long now that home would be the strange and frightening place.

Jorges went on to explain to Ben and I the necessity of preparing the grandmother for the difficulties of Manuel's homecoming. But she was a simple peasant; a letter would create more difficulties than it solved. Someone, it was clear, must go and see her and try to explain. 'But the village is at some distance, and the time, you understand—' He lifted his shoulders, flung out his hands and, white coat flapping, turned to go.

'Hey, just a minute!' Ben stopped him. 'Would it be any use my going in your place? You could prime me what to say to the grandmother.'

'You would do this favour for me, Ben, my friend?'

'Willingly,' Ben replied immediately, at his most charming, and if I were interested, he added, turning to me, my company on the journey would be most welcome. Would I like to come?

Like it? Nothing would have stopped me, really. A whole day, driving into the wild, mountainous heart of the island—what else but that prospect could have thrilled and excited me so? I agreed before wondering if Melissa might have need me, but when I approached her it appeared she didn't.

'Please,' she said, 'don't make me feel like a slave-driver! Anyway, I've plenty of work to do on my other thing. Look!' She took hold of my shoulders and swung me round to see my almost completed portrait, passionate fulfilment in her voice.

She had posed me with my back half-turned to her, looking over my shoulder, my hair loose. I couldn't know how others saw me, I'd no criterion to judge it by, but I could see that she had caught an essence rather than a likeness. It had what I supposed, from want of a more knowledgeable word, quality. Even I could see that.

'It's *lovely*' I said. 'It's sure to sell.'

'It already has! And guess who's bought it?—Ben. Don't look so astounded, he can afford it twenty times over. And now shoo! Off you go and enjoy yourself.'

Since we were to start out somewhere around mid-morning, I decided to fill in the time by putting in an hour or two at the clinic. It seemed I couldn't have decided better, as the morning turned out to be one of those that occur in every organisation, however well run.

I spent the first hour in a swim-suit with Constanca, working in the tiny heated indoor pool where the children spent part of their exercise routine. I enjoyed it myself, but from then on there wasn't a spare minute until the children's mid-morning break, when I staggered to a chair with a cup of coffee while they had a drink and biscuits.

Pedro, the large child who had been attacked by Manuel on my first visit to the clinic, had just had a plaster cast put on his malformed arm, to encourage the bones to grow correctly, and was being resentful and slightly tearful about it. I left him alone, watching as he attempted to carry biscuits and fruit juice to the table with only one hand, the other stuck out awkwardly in front of him. He would soon learn to cope with it. It astonished me just how quickly these children did adapt to the heaviest and most restricting appliances, but Pedro was not really a very bright child.

I waited until he'd finished eating and drinking, then I took my ballpoint pen from my pocket and went over to him. Watched by half a dozen solemn, intrigued faces, I wrote my name in block capitals on the plaster.

'There. That says "Christy",' I told Pedro, drawing a scroll round it with a flourish. It didn't take the others long to catch on, and then they were clamouring to fellow my example.

'No pushing!' I made my words explain themselves by marshalling the group into some sort of order while Pedro, now the centre of attraction, importantly held out his new status symbol.

'My turn next!'

I spun round and saw Ben standing in the doorway, watching the proceedings with amusement. 'You'll have to get in the queue then,' I replied, keeping my eye on the children milling around Pedro, intrigued by their new game.

I hoped, belatedly, that Jorges wouldn't object to what I'd done. He placed few restrictions as a rule, relying on good sense as to how we amused the children—which I hadn't so far found very difficult. They regarded me as a great comic diversion, laughing at my atrocious attempts at their language, calling me, 'Mees', and asking endless questions.

All but Manuel. He remained an unmanageable, introverted child. It was impossible to get through to him. Trouble rose like smoke when he was around. He stood now on the edge of the group surrounding Pedro, occasionally asserting himself by jostling one of the others with his elbow. Once or twice, he stepped forward, but then drew back at the last moment.

'Come on, Manuel, write your name. *Escreves o teu nome, Manuel.*' I took his arm, encouraging him forward, but he squirmed and shook it off, aiming a kick at my shins which fortunately missed. Casting me a furious look from under the brim of the ten-gallon hat, from which he refused to be parted, day or night, he turned and charged past Ben out of the room. Ben made no attempt to stop him, and I looked after him helplessly.

Ben said, 'Haven't they told you he can't read or write?'

'What? But that's incredible—he's one of the most intelligent children here.'

'I gather it's not so much can't as won't, poor little devil—part of his rebellion against everyone and everything. It's one of those chicken and egg situations. If he could read and write he'd gain the confidence in himself that he needs to face the world, but he needs to succeed at something before he'll learn.'

'I never knew how disturbed he was, but I've never been there when they have their lessons—I didn't realise. Oh heavens, have I made things worse!'

'Hardly that. With children like Manuel, it's one step forward and two back. According to Jorges, what he really needs is to make some special relationship with someone.'

'What about his grandmother, when he goes home?'

'Could be. But even if not, he won't be able to stay here indefinitely, there's too much demand for places.' He glanced at his watch. 'Are you nearly ready?'

'In a few minutes. I must just take Rosa's report to Jorges.'

'Cut along then. I'll keep an eye on this lot.'

*

The door of Jorges's study was, against custom, firmly shut, and, even more strangely, from within came raised voices—or one raised voice, that of Jorges himself. I couldn't make out the words, but the tone was unmistakable. I hesitated, but even as I did so, his voice stopped, and quietness ensued. I knocked rather loudly.

'*Enter*!'

I opened the door and walked into a heavy silence. Discord was strong in the air. The faces of both men in the room still registered a barely restrained anger. Jorges was standing by the window. His habit of running his fingers through his hair when disturbed had made it stand on end, like an angry cat's fur. His white coat was unbuttoned, both hands shoved deep into his trouser pockets.

'I'm sorry to disturb you—may I leave this?'

'Come in, Christy, Senhor Duente was just about to leave.' Jorges spoke with uncharacteristic coldness. 'Oh, you have not yet met?'

'We have spoken,' I said.

Jorges made the necessary introductions, and Alfonso Duente heaved himself out of the cane chair in front of the desk. It creaked as he stood up, saying, '*Muito prazer, senhorita*,' in that deep, grating voice I remembered so well. My senses had not played me false on that occasion. Now, as then, I felt something in him which made the hairs rise on my scalp.

He was a fat man whose shape an expensive tailor had done his best to disguise; his skin wore an unhealthy look, and the whites of his brown eyes held a yellowish tinge. His appearance was far from prepossessing, but it was something other, some nameless antipathy which induced in me this irrational sense of something to beware.

He stayed no longer than was necessary for common courtesy. It was obviously an effort for him to speak English, and Jorges made no attempt to help him out. When he had gone, there was a feeling of relief, of being able to breathe once more. He seemed to use up all the air in the room.

Jorges didn't immediately speak, peering into a cup on his desk that contained coffee long since cold. He suddenly drank it down in a gulp, like a man dying of thirst in the desert. His hands were not altogether steady. I handed him Rosa's report, watching him while he searched for a pen amongst the wildly chaotic rumpus on his desk.

By degrees, I liked to think our instant mutual liking for each other was developing into a warm friendship. You couldn't help being aware, working alongside him, of the rewards and satisfactions of a busy and fulfilled life, in its way as creative as Melissa's. Yet beneath the bubbling, exuberant exterior there was a sadness and soberness, invariably more evident after the visits of Caterina.

He never troubled to conceal the fact that he was in love with her, but she, in her attitude to Jorges, was habitually guarded, slightly defensive. She came to the clinic bearing gifts like a fairy godmother. Whether out of conscience regarding the children, or on the off chance of meeting Ben there, I could never make up my mind.

And now, this dissension between Jorges and Caterina's father, that had caused Jorges once more to lose his grip on himself, to show that anger of which, under his mild exterior, he was only too capable.

He rubbed a hand over his eyes, and I said, 'You work too hard. Don't you ever take time off?'

'Work too hard, my dear Christy?' he said, dwelling on the last syllable of my name, smiling faintly. 'Is not work that kills—but worry, eh? Especially over money, money...never borrow money is my advice to you. Debt is a rock around your neck that may one day drown you...Ah, here is the pen. You will wait for me to read?'

He read, signed and added a few comments, in spidery black handwriting. He handed it back, saying, 'A moment—' He went to a small pot on a shelf beneath a large crucifix hanging on the wall and removed a handful of *escudos* from it. 'A small present for you to give the grandmother of Manuel.'

As I took the money from him, I noticed that the shirt cuffs jutting from his coat were frayed, there was a button missing from the front.

*

The miles between the clinic and Manuel's village slid by without the need to talk much. The sort of scenic view that unrolled in front of us as we swept round mountains and dived down again was in any case the sort that left you running out of superlatives after the first few miles.

We passed through remote villages where tiny cottages had thatched roofs and the people were tough and wild-looking. The landscape was untamed and romantic, larger than life. Tree-sized heathers bloomed beside six-foot bilberries. Waterfalls dashed from a tremendous height. Sometimes, when the road dipped towards the coast, we went tunnelling under these, while the water crashed down. The black cliffs were a mile high, sheer to the rocks below. The beauty was heart-stopping, making you think of wild, passionate music...

And all the time, another note wove its own little melody...Duente, Melissa...Duente, Oliver...Duente, Jorges...

'Penny for them,' Ben broke into this unprofitable circling. 'Or are they worth more?'

'No, they're not! I was thinking of Senhor Duente, as a matter of fact. I met him for the first time this morning at the clinic.'

'Great for you!'

'You don't like him.'

'I wouldn't call him a bosom friend.'

'I didn't have the impression that he's a friend of Jorges's, either. In fact,' I added, watching his reaction, 'I'd go so far as to believe he's scared stiff of Duente.'

His brows drew together in a frown. 'That's going a bit far. Aren't you letting your imagination run away with you—again?'

'I don't think so,' I said quite sharply, stung by that 'again'. 'This morning they were having a ding-dong fight. I think it was about money—and I *know* he was frightened.'

'Money?' He drove on for a while before saying finally, 'Even supposing it's true—and I won't deny a lot of people may well have reason to be afraid of Duente—that's one business I'd strongly advise you to keep away from.'

I was willing enough to let the subject drop, not even to protest in my own defence that the last person I wanted to entangle with was Senhor Duente. Nor did I mention what was troubling me even more—Melissa's connection with him.

The hillside village was *en fête* when we arrived, with great ropes of pink and white paper flowers strung across the road, and deafening taped music played incessantly from loudspeakers. It was nearly impossible to drive up through the milling crowds.

'Damn, I'd forgotten it was a festival today,' Ben muttered as we crawled along, youths banging exuberantly against the car sides and tossing firecrackers in front of us. 'We'd better get out and walk.'

He manoeuvred the car into the side of the road and spoke to a man sweating behind a stall selling hot meat, bread and wine, pressing coins into his palm. '*Sim, senhor*—I will see that your car comes to no harm,' the man promised with a salute.

I took several photos, and then we turned to make our way up the street under the broiling sun. 'Oh, do look at those hats!' I pointed delightedly to a stall selling dolls in national costume, and piled high at one side with absurdly large straw hats.

'Tourist bait,' he remarked, smiling, but he knew I wanted one, and bought it despite my protests that I wasn't tall enough to wear it. He cupped my elbow and squeezed my arm against him. 'You're a nut!' he said, laughing into my face.

And my silly heart turned over with an uncomfortable lurch.

*

'So, he returns home, the little one?' Manuel's grandmother sat at the open door of her cottage, finishing off the embroidery of a huge tablecloth. We sat on a bench outside, sipping red wine. There was silence as the old woman wielded thin sharp scissors with incredible swiftness and precision, cutting away material between the intricacies of a leaf and flower design.

'Don't you ever cut the stitches?' I exclaimed, forgetting I couldn't be understood. Ben translated and the old woman smiled and shook her head—then her manner became serious and she began to speak to Ben in a rapid patois, to which I wasn't equal. She spoke for a long time, earnestly, with many gestures of her hands. Afterwards, when Ben was repeating to me the gist of what she'd said, her sharp black eyes never left our faces.

The sewing was second nature to her, she had told him. She could do much less than formerly, however, because her eyesight was growing bad, but she had to keep it up, since she had no other source of income. Her son had left—her youngest son, Manuel's father—to find work across the sea, like his brothers before him. Like them, she knew he would never come back. One day, perhaps, he would send for Manuel, but until then…

'Until then, it's she who has to pay for Manuel's keep?'

While the others had been speaking, I had had time to become aware of the bareness of the little house, whose entirety could be seen through the open door, its total lack of any comforts only too apparent. The old woman, who was probably nowhere near as old as she looked, wore cracked and patched shoes. Her clothes, though neat, were much mended. The glass of wine was obviously a richness of hospitality.

'It's not wholly the expense,' Ben said. 'She has dozens of grandchildren, and she has looked after them all, willingly, but this one, she says, is different. She's no longer quick enough, she hasn't the energy for looking after someone like Manuel.'

'I take her point! All the same, Ben...' 'His accident was caused when he ran out into the road and pretended to fall in front of a tourist's car. It's an old trick, to stop the motorist so that the child can beg money—only this time the driver couldn't stop quickly enough. Since then, the grandmother feels the responsibility is too great.'

He turned back to the old woman and they talked for some time longer. When we finally stood up to take our leave, she accepted my halting thanks for the wine and the envelope from Jorges with equal graciousness. We shook hands, and Ben let his hand rest momentarily on her shoulder. There were tears in her eyes as she murmured, '*Adeus*!'

The look she gave him seemed frighteningly trustful. We were to cut back through the centre of the island for the return journey, but first, Ben suggested lunch at a restaurant he knew, where the tables were set outside, overlooking the sea. I'd been warned to take a sweater, and was glad of it. Despite the heat of the sun, the air was bracing and keen. We were the only customers on the terrace overlooking the sea.

I was healthily hungry, and finally settled for an omelette and some wine. When we were drinking our coffee, Ben said, leaning back in his chair, 'Something will be done for Manuel, you know. If it's any consolation to you. I've already had one or two thoughts on the subject. We'll find some way of getting him out of his trouble.'

'Oh, Ben!'

He grinned. 'Universal uncle, that's me.' I looked at him, this—this Casanova, this moody, quick-tempered, impatient man, who had women at his feet just because he was so good-looking. And maybe, I suddenly found myself admitting, because he had on the credit side a host of qualities I couldn't begin to name...yet I couldn't quite bring myself to trust him entirely.

A Handful of Shadows

I turned my glance towards him and his eyes met mine, all at once dark and serious, looking at me with an unreadable expression. I had to look away. Blindly, I reached out to touch the pink-flushed petals of a creamy oleander, its clusters overhanging the wall near me. In my hot confusion, my elbow caught the edge of my bag, sending it spinning from the table, scattering its entire bulging contents, and giving me respite as I went on my knees to pick them up.

He chased after a lipstick, stamped on an old envelope to prevent the wind catching it, retrieved a handful of loose coins, several ballpoints, a packet of tissues, a roll of mints. 'Here you are—everything but the kitchen sink, though I'm afraid this appears to have been broken.'

'It was broken before,' I told him, and so was the magic of the day, as I looked at the photograph of Dave that he held.

I'd forgotten to have the glass replaced in Funchal after all, though it had been tucked into a pocket of my bag ever since I'd found it smashed on the floor of my bedroom. Ben put it on the table between us and I wondered how I could so easily have pushed everything into the back of my mind.

'Do you believe in poltergeists, Ben?' I asked.

He gave me a sharp, considering look, then leaned back. 'The straight answer's no. Though I'd rather believe in them than in some person deliberately smashing things. This the latest catastrophe?'

I nodded and told him what had happened. He listened intently, his eyes on the photo as I spoke, but when I'd finished he said carelessly, 'I shouldn't worry about it. You're probably right about the wind—or Josefina. Who is he, by the way?' He tapped the frame.

'Oh, his name's Dave. We were students together.' I glanced at the familiar features, feeling my colour rise as he watched me. 'Well, that's what I thought myself at first, about the wind, but now—I'm not so sure.'

'You'd be making a big mistake,' he observed, ignoring the last part of what I said, indicating the photo as I put it back in my bag. 'Young David there's not for you. Too self-centred, I'd say. Too immature.'

Annoyed, I said, 'How can you possibly know? But never mind that. What's more important is that somebody was getting at Melissa through me.'

'Oh?' He rocked his chair on its two back legs. 'And why should anyone want to do that?' he asked, deliberately bland.

'I don't know—but I'm dead certain that it all harks back to Oliver, and his accident. Only it wasn't, was it? I think he committed suicide, and the reason he did so is all tied up with why Melissa is so unhappy now.'

'For Pete's sake, I thought we'd finished with all that!'

'Did you? Then I'd better tell you, if something bothers me I'll stay with it...'

'To the bitter end?'

Abruptly, he left his chair and went to lean against the railings at the end of the terrace, his back to me, looking down. The breeze ruffled his blond hair, filled out his thin shirt like a sail.

He came back and poured more coffee. 'Let me tell you something,' he said, 'about the first settlers here. They set fire to the forest that covered the entire island in order to clear it—but the fire got out of hand. They couldn't stop what they had started. It's said the fire burned continuously for seven years.'

'I know. And according to Dee, the ashes made the island one of the most fertile in the world.'

'Christy, I'm only trying to warn you—don't start something you can't stop.'

I said, rather fast, 'Isn't it better that I know the truth—rather than guess and put my own interpretation on things? It's not idle curiosity, you must know that. Melissa is in very serious trouble. I just know it—and I don't really think I can bear it.' The last words came in a rush because, very suddenly, I heard my voice beginning to shake.

He looked at me in silence, and there was something in his gaze that warmed and held me as if a cloak had been thrown round my shoulders. 'All right then,' he said softly, 'I'll tell you what I know. Then maybe you'll be convinced that there was nothing at all to prove Oliver's death wasn't an accident. There have been other accidents up there, plenty.'

'But?' I interrupted him.

'But nothing. He was an experienced climber—all sports appealed to him, swimming, sailing. He had a magnificent physique for a man of his age and he always took care to keep himself very fit.'

Oliver, self-confident, bronzed and smiling in the photograph in Dee's room, a man careful of himself in every sense of the word. 'There you are, then! If he was an experienced climber, he wouldn't have gone blundering about in the mist.'

'Maybe he just slipped. People do, even those who should know better. And there was a lot of cloud that day.'

'But you don't believe that, do you? You believe it *was* suicide.'

He considered me for a few moments, then shook his head. 'No, it won't do. You never met our Oliver, did you? He was the complete extrovert—hail-fellow-well-met, not the type to take his own life. There are always signs—you can tell, if you're aware enough.'

Fleetingly, his face was wintry. A bleak, inward look that took all the animation from his face. It was possible to see how he might look when he was an old man. I was once more on the verge of remembering what had been puzzling me about him, but now, inexplicably, I didn't want to. I pushed away the swift flash of memory, and when he spoke again it was gone, like the expression on his face. 'Why should he take his own life anyway?' he said. 'He had everything going for him—a beautiful, talented wife, his health—he enjoyed life…'

'He was rich,' I said, deliberately.

He met my look steadily, then shrugged in an uncommitted way. 'As you say. Wealthy art-dealer with a penthouse in New York, holiday home here on Madeira, sea-going yacht, the lot. A few days before he died, he was talking to me, as excited as a kid with a toffee apple, about a deal he was about to bring off with Duente.'

'Oh? What sort of deal?'

'He didn't say, something tremendous, I'd guess. I've been trying to get it out of Caterina for weeks. She swears her father never told her and maybe he didn't. Or maybe she doesn't want to admit what she suspects. So you see, Christy, what it all adds up to—it *had* to be an accident.'

There was a profound silence. Fear that had lain dormant at the back of my mind stirred and began to come painfully awake. My voice spoke of its own accord.

'You don't believe it was suicide—I don't see how it could have been an accident. There is, however, another possibility.'

He scraped back his chair and stood leaning over me, his hands flat on the table. He said softly, 'Stop it, Christy! Stop it. Accident, suicide, that's one thing. But murder's another. If folk go around suggesting it, sooner or later someone's going to believe it.'

*

There was half-an-hour still before the evening meal, and no one was about yet when I went downstairs. The rooms met me with secret silence. I longed for voices, ordinary, everyday conversation—yet I knew that meeting the others, with all my new suspicions, would be like walking into an entanglement of barbed wire.

Restless, I walked out into the garden, where the plants and trees were already losing their colour, absorbing the darkness into themselves. By the time I reached the waterfall pool, the shadows were gathering swiftly, the woods behind crouching like a huge spider. Even my pretty, friendly pool looked ominous and secretive, and, remembering the rocks above, I shuddered.

A white creeper rippled with almost sinister abundance over a rock. I stood examining its cool petals; the waterfall's splash absorbed the approaching footsteps. He seemed to materialise out of the shadows, a tall figure looming up on me. I turned a startled face towards him when he greeted me softly.

'Ben! I didn't hear you coming.'

'I've been here some time, watching you. It's called a Moon Goddess,' he said, touching the creeper. 'A night blossom, rare at this altitude, but it's a sheltered spot. You could be the Moon Goddess yourself in that white dress—but on second thoughts, it isn't your setting. You should have the sun shining on your hair.'

I was silent, remembering with vivid clarity that it was here in this very clearing that I had overheard that exchange between him and Melissa.

'I knew I'd find you here,' he went on. 'I'd like to talk to you, now that you've had time to think.'

'What more is there to say?'

'I've an apology to make for a start. Today hasn't turned out as I intended. I'm sorry it was spoiled. An attractive girl like you should be having fun, not letting yourself in for a lot of needless hassle.'

'Don't, Ben, this is serious.'

'I'm always serious when I'm asking a girl out to eat and dance. What about it? Forget all this for a bit.'

For a moment, I thought how wonderful it would be, a great lifting of the weight that seemed to have settled on my shoulder, but—'Forget? How can I forget?'

'Discipline, child, discipline!' His voice was light and teasing and I was meant to respond. He was making it difficult to maintain the reality of what had passed between us this afternoon, but I disliked the thought that I was being manipulated, that my own feeling of being overwhelmed by things too deep for me to understand and cope with was being played on.

It was no consolation that, as he had predicted, I didn't like what I'd learned through my persistence. Moreover, there was something else, some further dread that lurked in the deep recesses of my mind, and unconsciously, I fought against the knowledge.

He took hold of my hand. 'I'm only asking you to bide your time.' The breeze rustled the trees, and I might almost have imagined the next words, so softly did he speak them. 'Trust me, Christy. There could be danger if you don't.'

It occurred to me there could be more danger if I did. He was the last person I ought to trust in my present frame of mind. I was not entirely in control of myself when he was around at the best of times. I half-turned away from him, and heard a sound, subtly different from the other night movements around us. I spun round, but there was darkness, and silence save for the rustling of the shrubs, the fall of water.

'What's the matter?'

'I thought I heard someone.'

'No one there. Some animal perhaps.'

I turned back to him and made one last effort. 'Look, I know how much you care about Melissa...'

He said softly, 'She isn't the only one. I care about you.' Before I knew what was happening, I was in his arms. 'Oh yes, I care about you, Christy. I think I might even be going to love you.'

Love me? He attracted me and frightened me at the same time. He kept secrets from me. How could he love me?

He bent his head and put his lips to mine. And I was boneless, melting into the long, deep kiss between us. And who knows what might have happened then, if I hadn't, at that totally inappropriate moment, remembered the thing about him for which I had searched my memory in vain.

Sick at myself, I pushed against his chest.

'Christy?'

'I must go.'

'Go? I thought you were coming out with me?'

'Some other time, Ben.'

'Oh, by all means let's make it some other time,' he said coldly, and I turned away because I couldn't bear to look at the frozen mask of his face.

I ran almost blindly down the path and nearly ran into Marian Lopes at the intersection with the main one.

She was too flustered, unduly put out at the meeting, to notice my agitation, and some of her uncompromising attitude was lost in a breathless explanation of why she'd been up to the studio. 'I sometimes slip up there of an evening to do some tidying up, and I'd a bit of spare time tonight, so…maybe you won't mention it, though. She'd prefer me to leave things as they are.'

It wasn't the first time I'd notice Marian never referred to Melissa by name if she could help it. She added, 'But you can't just leave everything to gather dust, can you?'

Why not, if that was how Melissa wanted it? What right had Marian to decree otherwise? And as I thought about that, one or two other questions occurred to me. Had it been Marian creeping past the pool on her way to the studio a few minutes ago? Why had she thought it necessary to keep herself hidden? Why, unless she was eavesdropping? That wasn't a thing anyone would like to admit, especially this strange, cold woman with her stiff sense of right and wrong.

*

The shrill, insistent telephone dragged me, protesting, from fathoms down. I sat up, still dazed from the deep sleep into which I'd fallen after lunch. The ringing stopped and I fell back against the cushions of the cane chair and closed my eyes again. Then memory came flooding back.

Yesterday had been grim—though not by any means all of it. Parts would stay with me for ever, shining and precious; they were the ones I would remember, not the rest. I'd been able to get through supper by talking generally of what had interested me about my trip, though I'd been aware of Melissa's eyes registering puzzlement, and I knew she guessed something had gone wrong.

And today, for the first time since I'd been working at the clinic, I'd been glad to leave when lunch time came. I'd been at everyone's beck and call. All the jobs I liked least were there to be done, and I'd made heavy weather of them. There hadn't even been time for a break. The only consolation was that my lively group had been quiet and good, and I hoped for the sake of the staff dealing with them this afternoon that it wasn't the lull before the storm.

'It's Miss Duente on the phone.' I opened my eyes, and saw Marian beckoning me from the French window.

'Oh, it's you,' Caterina said unflatteringly as I picked up the receiver. 'Well, thank

goodness I've got through to someone. The line between here and the clinic is out of order again. You'd think, with all the money we paid to have it installed...'

'Can I do anything for you?' I asked, still muzzy from sleep.

'Ye-es, I suppose you can. I have a boy here who says his name's Manuel, an odd little character in a Stetson who's run away from the clinic.'

'What?' Jerked into full wakefulness, I saw in a flash the reason for the children's unusual quietness this morning. All was explained. Manuel hadn't been there to stir up trouble.

'He tried to commit suicide under my car wheels. At least that's what it looked like—until he started begging for money. He finally admitted he wanted it to board ship in Funchal and go to his father.' 'Oh, poor little soul! Look, Jorges will be worried sick about him. He's sure to have been missed by now. You'd better get him back there.'

There was a pause at the other end. 'I know that, but he refuses to go. He's afraid they're going to send him away—which I suppose is logic of a kind—but I don't think I can force him back. I'd rather face a tiger. And I daren't leave him while I go and tell Jorges he's here.' I waited for what I guessed was coming. 'Er—Ben's always telling me you're a wow with the kids, so do you think...?'

I thought quickly. 'All right. If I can get through to Jorges, I'll set his mind at rest, then I'd better come over, though I'll warn you, *nobody's* a wow with Manuel!'

His absence had just been discovered, and the whole clinic was in a state, looking for him. Jorges's relief was boundless when I managed to get through and assure him the boy was safe. When I told him where, there was silence at the other end of the line. Then, surprisingly, he gave a satisfied chuckle, but refused to explain the reason for this amusement.

I walked up the road and turned off to climb the half-mile or so of twisting drive that led to the Duente residence, perched precariously high on the rocks, wondering what good I was going to be able to do when I got there.

I found Caterina listening to loud pop music from a transistor radio beside her. She lay stretched decoratively along a cushioned lounger set on the terrace, which ran the whole length of the house front, and from which the rest of the property dropped dramatically. There was no garden as such, though huge tubs of scarlet canna lilies stood along the terrace, and the white walls were clothed in a variety of brilliant, hot-coloured climbers.

Caterina's car was parked by the front door, near which she lay, sunbathing. As I neared the car, a black cowboy hat became visible above the top of the steering wheel, a pair of suspicious little black eyes peered through. Of the rest of Manuel, nothing could be seen.

Caterina sat up, beckoning me to a chair, poured me a tall glass of iced lime juice from a vacuum jug and thrust it at me. She turned off the radio and from the car a series of racing-car noises could be heard.

'Are you sure he's all right in there?' I asked nervously, gratefully sipping the cold, refreshing drink.

Caterina raised her elegant eyebrows. 'He won't touch anything. He's promised, haven't you, Manuel?' she demanded, raising her voice and repeating the question in Portuguese. He stuck his head out of the window to give me an affronted look that was the exact replica of Caterina's. They looked laughably alike.

'So what's to be done with the child?' she asked after listening to what I could tell her of Manuel's history and circumstances.

'Well, I was thinking,' I began, when she cut me short.

'He can't stay here, that's certain.'

'Your father would object?'

'Certainly not—if I wished it. But I don't.' She drank the rest of her lime juice and lay back against the cushions. She was wearing a white sundress that set off her olive colouring, and huge sunglasses, so that her expression was impossible to read. 'Has Jorges suggested this?' she asked suddenly.

'No, why should he? I just thought Manuel seems to have taken a liking to you, and for the time being...'

She interrupted, saying in a bored voice, 'It wouldn't have surprised me. Jorges is always trying to inveigle me into helping him out. He will never admit that people need a little fun—everyone's entire being isn't bounded by those kids. It's a pity he's not more like Ben.'

From inside the house came the rattle of Dee's typewriter keys. Siesta time was obviously not for her. I looked at Caterina lounging with her arms crossed behind her head and wondered what she did with herself all day long. With my usual lack of caution, I said, 'Do *you* have fun, Caterina, with what you're doing with your life?' She took her sunglasses off and regarded me with a long, unblinking stare. 'I'm sorry,' I said, 'I shouldn't have said that. Please forget it. I suppose I asked because it's something to do with what I'm trying to work out for myself.'

She swung her legs to the ground and abruptly went to lean on the terrace wall, her back to me, reminding me of Ben's identical action yesterday. 'If you must know,' she said over her shoulders, 'no, I don't. Sometimes, I'm bored, bored, bored!'

She came back and flung herself full length on to the lounger, closing her eyes. 'But there's nothing else I want to do, either, not passionately, not enough to do anything about it. You wouldn't understand.'

'I think I might.'

When there was the world to choose from, there was too much choice. People like Melissa, like Jorges, who had one consuming ambition, they were the lucky ones, their choice was made for them.

'And please don't suggest helping at the clinic,' she went on scornfully. 'I'm squeamish about illness of any kind, I really cannot bear it. The thought of doing things for those kids…I'm sorry, I just couldn't.'

She reached out her slender arm and pushed a bell set in the wall. A maid appeared and Caterina held out the jug, rudely, without bothering to speak. When the girl had gone, she turned the knob of the transistor once more and the brash music split the calm.

Squeamish maybe—at the thought of committing herself to marriage with a poor, hard-working doctor? Was wealth so important to her? She had obviously been used to it all her pampered life.

At this point we were joined by Dee, unruffled and cool as an iceberg in pale blue, as if she hadn't spent half the day over the typewriter. She came bringing the refilled jug, which she set on the table. 'Caterina told me you were coming over here, Christy. I'm through for today. I didn't bring the car, so I'll walk back with you when you're ready.' She nodded towards Caterina's car, from which Manuel was climbing. 'Has the runaway's fate been decided yet?'

I hesitated rather miserably, but before I could answer, Caterina sat up, turning the radio off again and saying ungraciously, 'Oh, well, I guess he'll have to stay here—but only until Jorges has decided what to do with him.'

She accepted my relieved thanks in such an off-hand manner I felt sorry I'd made them, until I saw her reach out and throw a careless hand round Manuel's shoulders. An unexpected stab of pity for her smote me, a small part of my antipathy began to dissolve. Caterina was spoiled, impossible, but not altogether irredeemable.

Dee was smiling, looking at her watch. 'I've left the letters for your father to sign. He and his visitor seem to be making a day of it. Maybe you'll tell him…'

'I think Mr Halliday is leaving by the evening plane, but you can tell Papa yourself. Here he is.'

Senhor Duente had emerged through the French windows and was making his ponderous way along the terrace, accompanied by a nondescript, middle-aged man wearing a neat blazer and light-weight trousers.

Duente made the introductions. 'You have met my daughter—' for a moment his huge paw rested, heavily affectionate, on Caterina's shoulder—'my secretary, Miss Newman, and Miss Durrant…my new partner, Mr Prentiss Halliday, of Florida.'

Mr Halliday's greeting was charming and polite, his smile wide, his eyes so sharp and shrewd that I suspected he might well have a computer in place of a heart. At the same time, he looked far too negative a little man to cause Dee to react to him as she did, with every appearance of shock.

Nothing else, surely, could have made her lose her colour so rapidly, made her so agitated that her usual calm and poise entirely deserted her. With hastily undignified goodbyes, she fled with me down the drive.

I noticed vaguely that something was out of place as we walked into the drive of the Quinta, but I was too bothered to give it much thought.

How strange Dee's conduct had been—how uncharacteristic! Was it an unwelcome recognition of Mr Halliday that had so upset her? Certainly, he himself had given no indication of ever having met her previously, or registered anything but pleasantness. It puzzled me, but since she gave no explanation and hurried off to her room as soon as we reached the house, I was left still mystified by her behaviour as I went up to the studio for what would possibly be my last sitting.

The big, bright, sun-filled studio was empty, but couldn't have been so for long. Instant coffee powder was ready in a mug beside the small primus, the kettle was boiling its head off. I looked around the studio, stacked with all the paraphernalia of a painter's workroom, and saw other evidence of abandonment.

A brush loaded with burnt umber was left unforgivably uncleaned on the palette, the abstract on which she'd been working was left uncovered. A biscuit crunched under my foot as I moved, one of a whole packet which had been spilled and left where they fell. As I bent to retrieve them, I saw the note, lying on the floor as if it had fluttered from nerveless fingers.

I sank down on to the bright Spanish blanket that covered the low divan, staring at the thing with sick disgust.

Pale blue, common-or-garden writing paper, the message written in black felt pen, the characters so shaky they must have been written with the left hand in an attempt at disguise. Someone had an appetite for bad detective fiction. There were just five words scrawled on it: *How did Oliver Newman die?*

I sat looking at it for a long time.

An acrid smell filled the air, the kettle had boiled itself dry. I leaped up to turn the stove off. Where was Melissa? Then I remembered what it was that had struck me as odd when I'd returned from the Duente house with Dee. Her car had been missing from its usual place at the bottom of the drive.

I raced out of the studio and down to the house, bursting in on Marian and Josefina, who were cleaning silver. Josefina shook her head in answer to my question, but Marian said yes, she had heard the car, and seen it leave from an upstairs window.

'Did you notice which way she went?'

'Left,' she said positively, intent on polishing spoons.

That way, the road led upwards. Either to the Duente house—and Melissa hadn't gone there, otherwise Dee and I must have passed her—to the clinic, which was a possibility...or up to the top slopes of the volcano, to the fateful Pico do Aeriero.

Without wasting time on further questions, I left them.

'Come in and join me,' Ben said, waving the coffee pot, after a moment in which I knew we were both painfully remembering the moment in the garden the night before. 'I've just come down from the clinic, and what with all the hoo-ha over Manuel I felt I needed—' He broke off abruptly. 'What's the matter?'

'Melissa. She's gone, taken her car. Up the road—not to the Duentes, I've just come from there, nor the clinic—I've rung, and she's not there either. Ben—I think she must have driven up to the volcano.'

He became absolutely still. 'What makes you think that?' he asked, all at once very quiet and attentive, putting the coffee pot down with precision.

I told him what Marian had said, and handed him the letter, taking it with loathing from my pocket. 'I found—this, in the studio. I guess the other letters must have said something similar.'

'The other letters, Christy?'

'You didn't *know* about them? Three or four, I think.'

'No, I didn't.' He became so lost in his thoughts that for a while I hardly dared to interrupt. But time was passing. I had to remind him. I said urgently, 'Ben, you know how she drives.'

He said simply, 'Let's go.'

CHAPTER IV

'This is the end of the road, Christy.'

It might have been the end of the world. The route had ascended higher and higher, becoming ever more precipitous. Pine and eucalyptus had given way to broom, heather and spiny ilex. Now there was scarcely any vegetation at all. We had entered a strange, unworldly landscape, and stretching before us the jagged ground was blue-grey and cinder red, as if the volcanic eruptions which had created it had barely cooled.

Deep gullies and vertical ravines dropped a couple of thousand feet either side into swirling cloud, where intrepid mountain sheep maintained a foothold on perilous crannies, seeking grass. Down an opposite slope a molten lava flow of un-guessable age was still discernible. It was sharply cold as we climbed out of the car on to a levelled patch of ground where vehicles could park and turn round.

Ben threw me a thick sweater from the back seat and he himself donned an anorak. A coachload of noisy German tourists, preparing to leave, waved jolly encouragements, pointing to a high, narrow ridge where possibly one might teeter along a path between two craters. There was no sign at all of Melissa's, or any other, car. 'So she can't have come here,' Ben said.

The coach revved up, shatteringly, and moved off. The groaning of its engine grew fainter, faded altogether. The silence was total, save for the faint, plaintive bleat of a sheep from miles below. 'Perhaps she parked the car elsewhere, and walked.' My voice rang loudly in the eerie emptiness. I knew there had been nowhere for miles where a car could have been left undetected.

Ben stuck his hands in his pockets, kicking at the loose stones at his feet. 'We've got this all wrong. Why should Melissa have come up here?'

'There's nowhere else she could have gone. Marian said she turned left—up the road.'

'If Marian wasn't mistaken.'

Marian didn't make mistakes like that, and we both knew it. Deliberately misleading then? Suspicion returned—my encounter with her the previous evening, coming from the studio—her unease. What more likely than that she had gone there to plant the letter where Melissa was sure to find it? She was uptight, frustrated—the type one could all too easily imagine bearing grudge enough to write those beastly letters.

Marian was jealous enough of Melissa, and had had ample opportunity to have played those childish, yet horrible and sinister tricks, too...

'Let's think this out,' Ben was saying. 'What would you have done in Melissa's position? Would you have come chasing up here? If you received a letter like that, who would you run to?'

I had run to him when I found Melissa gone. Blindly, without thought of doubt, or suspicion. In that moment, I had obeyed my instincts.

He said, 'It's my bet she went straight down to Felipe.'

Instinct again told me he was right. Yet she hadn't shown Felipe the other letters, so why this? She had her own reasons for keeping her secrets from him. Unless she had changed her mind. One thing was, however, certain: she wasn't here.

I made myself relax, leaning against the car bonnet. But the stillness of the place, the clouds boiling down there below, the probability that here someone had killed Oliver Newman, made it impossible. I shivered. 'It's weird up here, isn't it?'

He nodded and threw a swift glance at me. 'The panic's over,' he said. 'Melissa's safe. It's a pity not to see the rest while you're here. It's an experience that shouldn't be missed. Walk along there,' he said, pointing, 'and you'll come to the highest spot on the island. From it you can see the real volcanic centre where it all began, aeons ago.'

I gazed with something approaching horror at that terrible ridge that seemed to run along the top of the world, at the craters dropping to either side.

'It's perfectly safe. Look, there's even a handrail, for part of the way, anyway.'

But the track was loose and shaly; it disappeared altogether in places. And either side, those mind-numbing drops. The other side of the valley was in sun, here it was in deep shade, cold and menacing. I swallowed. Fear was all in the mind...and Ben was here. *Ben was here.*

A girl had taken her life because of him. A man had died on this spot. I had last night thrown Ben Battista's love back in his face. Instinct was no armour against this deadly, creeping suspicion. I knew a moment of despair and disillusion, before common sense reasserted itself.

I took a step forward and he smiled. I followed him, tentatively, because my sandals gave a poor grip on the slithering surface. It was highly optimistic to have thought I was going to see much, concentrating as I must on watching every step I trod. I couldn't even rely on the handrail, which seemed more a matter of encouragement than aid, since the support posts themselves were often wobbly.

And then, without warning, the path was no longer there. It had worn away for a distance of a couple of feet. To bridge that distance by a single stride was feasible—Ben had done it without thinking—but not I. I stood riveted to the spot, licking dry lips.

'Ben,' I croaked, hardly above a whisper, but in that still air he heard me and turned. For a long moment we faced each other, and more than the break in the path divided us. Then he smiled again.

He came back towards me along the path, edging nearer with every step, his eyes never leaving my face, hypnotising me like a snake with its prey. He said softly, 'Don't move, Christy. Don't try to move.'

It was a totally unnecessary command. My muscles were locked, paralysed by the fear that I might sidestep to get away from him and fall headlong to my death. I stood transfixed until his hands reached out and touched me, took my arms without haste in a grip from which there was no escape.

'Of all the lunatic, crazy things to do,' he shouted at me when we were back in the car, furious as he pulled a flask from the glove compartment and screwed off the cap. 'Here, drink this. Why didn't you just tell me you were scared of heights?'

I shook my head and found I was trembling too violently to drink. He noticed it and held the flask steady in my frozen hands. I drank the brandy and felt better at once.

'Christy. Christy.' He took the flask from me and held my hands between his to warm them. 'And that other time—when you went down to rescue Heathcliff—it wasn't just ordinary fright?'

His tenderness now, everything else forgotten, was too much for me. I couldn't bear it. 'Why—why did you take me along there?'

'I simply wanted you to see, and admit, just how easy it is to fall, how fatally easy. I wanted you to believe it, once and for all. But I wouldn't have dreamed of it if I'd known. What an idiot you are! Heaven knows, I've seen fright on faces before, but never have I seen such a look of abject terror.'

'I was scared out of my mind,' I could admit now, and began to shake again. That moment when his arms had closed round me...

'*You* were scared! And so you should have been—I thought you were going to topple sideways from sheer fright.'

'I nearly did.'

Some guarded quality in my voice perhaps arrested him. He gave me a long, searching look. 'Ye gods,' he said quietly, 'you thought—that—of me. You thought I'd harm you?' He let go of my hands as though they burned him.

'No,' I said, 'no!' But I had. For a moment, I had.

I could see he was savagely angry, and I kept my own silence on the way back. By the time we drove through the gates, however, he was in total command of himself. He had learned control in the disciplined vocation of racing that had been his chosen career—and, in any case, I had learned that his anger was the sort that easily dissipates. But I was uneasily aware that maybe I had driven the tip of the wedge just too far into the relationship that could have been growing between us.

Melissa's car was in its usual place. 'See, nothing to worry about, after all,' he pointed out.

We walked on and came to a halt on the back terrace. Dee's bedroom window was wide open and her record player on. Rachmaninov poured out into the garden like golden syrup. 'There's still the matter of the letter,' I said.

'So there is.'

The kitchen door opened and Marian came out. 'Oh, there you are! Sorry you had a wasted journey. She apparently changed her mind when she'd gone a few yards up the road and turned back into Funchal to see her husband.'

A sly little smile lurked on her face, adding to my growing conviction that my suspicions about her could not be wholly unfounded.

'Where is Senhora Battista now?' Ben asked. 'In the studio? OK, Christy. Come on.'

'So it was you who found the letter!' Melissa said. 'I knew someone must have. Careless of me, I should have burned it like the others.'

'Why? Why burn the evidence that ever existed?' I said.

She moved competently round the room, finishing off her interrupted work. Reaching out with familiarity for the things she needed, on her own ground, working with absorbed concentration, I could almost have believed I had imagined the abandonment, the air of desolation I had felt so strongly in this room not an hour before.

She scrubbed vigorously at her palette with a knife. 'And what would that have proved? Clever little Melissa, writing anonymous letters to herself, inventing a persecution complex, breaking up the happy home—all because she's going through a bad patch in her work and must blame something?' She threw a cloth over her work, dunked brushes in a jar and wiped them carefully on a rag. 'That's what they all believe, you know.'

'Not me,' Ben said tightly, 'since I didn't know about the letters. Why didn't you tell me? It would have made all the difference.'

'Oh, well—' she said evasively and then, her voice shaking, 'it's all nonsense, of course.'

'Of course it is!' I said roundly. 'And this foul letter proves it. Have they all been like this?'

'Not exactly. In one way or another, they all told me to get out, go away—or else. I suppose this constitutes the "or else".'

'Did they indeed?' Ben said. They looked at each other, while I tried and failed to interpret the swift current of meaning which flashed between them.

'Only a lunatic would believe you'd write this sort of thing to yourself,' I said. 'Why should you want to raise questions about the way Oliver died—or,' I added slowly, 'hush it up, for that matter?'

Ben walked across to the easel supporting my picture—his picture too now, I supposed—and stood looking at it, his hands in his pockets. Melissa came to perch on the divan beside me, studying my face. 'Hush it up? Well, yes, I might want to do that,' she said in a high, nervous voice that caused Ben to spin round.

'Melissa—be careful!'

She smiled crookedly at him, shook her head and went on, 'I do know how Oliver died. I was the one who killed him.'

Maybe the shock I'd received up there on the volcano had anaesthetised me to the extent where I couldn't take in this further one. I stared blankly out of the window, vaguely surprised to see that everything looked normal.

A leaf rustled against the window. I jumped as I felt Melissa's feather-light touch on my arm. 'I should have broken it more gently.'

Did she truly imagine that was possible? That there was anything gentle at all about the fact of murder? My mind fumbled around it, seeking a way out. I said, speaking to her but including Ben, 'I think I ought to tell you

I've already heard about the way Oliver died, and that everyone insists it was due to an accidental fall.' I turned to Ben, but his back was to the light so that I couldn't see the expression on his face.

'I know they do.' Her voice was shaking. 'But it wasn't so. What I've just said was true. Oh, I didn't actually push him over the edge, not literally. Though I might just as well have done.'

She stopped, rubbing at a smear of paint on her thumb, and I sagged with relief. Ben said nothing.

'I shouldn't ever have married Oliver, you know,' she went on in a rush. 'I began to realise that almost immediately—but he'd always been so marvellous before, and I owed him—everything. He launched me, made my name known, got me commissions, everything he was so good at.'

'That's one heck of a reason for marrying anybody!' Ben broke in, roughly sardonic.

'It didn't take me long to find that out, either, but it wouldn't have been so bad if he'd stuck to what he could do. Only it wasn't exciting enough for him, you see—he was a gambler by nature ... ' Her voice faltered, and I put my arm round her shoulders and squeezed.

'No, let me go on, Christy. I want both of you to know.'

She had held herself in check for so long that the words came tumbling out now in an effort to explain what had led up to the tragedy. It was fairly incoherent, but I managed to grasp the relevant facts.

It had all come to a head, she said, when Oliver began to suggest leaving Madeira. The quiet, uneventful island life was totally unsuited to a man of his temperament, made him restless and dissatisfied. But to leave the island was the last thing Melissa wanted. By then she had met Felipe. 'We met in secret,' she admitted, 'though we were never lovers. Felipe is honourable about such things; about divorce, too, in fact.'

Then suddenly Oliver had become fired with yet another of his plots for making money. 'You know how he was, Ben,' she said.

'Uh-huh, I know. Always looking for something that would make him rich overnight, the gold at the end of the rainbow.'

'Well, this time he was sure he'd found it. He told me he was taking a trip to New York to raise the necessary capital. But he wasn't able to…it was a terrible blow to his ego when at last he had to admit himself defeated. He telephoned me and he sounded frightful, depressed and in a sort of rage with everybody, including himself. He told me we should have to sell this house and take a rented apartment in the States somewhere. I was desperate. I knew I should have to ask him for a divorce, now. The day before he was due home, I wrote Felipe a note which Emilio was to deliver, asking him to meet me on the Pico do Aeriero.'

'What?'

'Ben, I know it sounds dramatic,' she said defensively, 'but I thought, nobody goes there except tourists. Anyway, there was no need to send the note — Felipe drove up to see you that morning, didn't he?'

'I remember—and I saw you talking to him after he'd left me.'

'We couldn't say much, but he didn't think a lot of my suggested meeting place, either. In the end, we met down at the Botanical Gardens. Only, you see, I forgot about destroying the note, Oliver came home while I was meeting Felipe, a day before he was expected, must have found it and gone up to the top expecting to find us together.'

Silence stretched between us.

'You really should be more careful, leaving your correspondence lying around!' Ben remarked at last, with unnecessary flippancy. But he had a strange, excited look on his face, bright-eyed and dangerous. I felt rather sick.

Something was wrong with Melissa's argument. Was it feasible that a man would throw himself off the edge of a mountain just because he'd found out his wife was having an affair, especially a man such as Oliver Newman appeared to have been?

'I know what you're thinking, Christy,' Melissa said, 'but he just couldn't have slipped! He was far too careful of himself for that. If Oliver went over the edge, he did it deliberately. He never did *anything* without reason—and he hated it if I looked at another man. And having seen my letter—' She flushed and admitted, 'I—wasn't very discreet. Imagine, the mood he was in, then finding out about Felipe! And whether he slipped or jumped, I'm still morally responsible. He wouldn't have been there but for me.'

'Maybe,' I said, but thinking someone was implying more than moral responsibility.

She said slowly, 'He must have found my note, otherwise why should he set out up there after a long and tiring flight from New York? The thing is, though, the note wasn't on his body, and I never found it afterwards. I told myself Oliver must have destroyed it before he went out, but that wasn't very likely, was it? So maybe he didn't find it, maybe someone else did, and showed it to him.'

'And the only person who can give you an alibi,' Ben said, 'is your husband, Felipe.'

Melissa began to walk about the room. Heathcliff came out of his basket in the corner and followed her, whimpering. She picked him up and hugged him to her breast as if she were very cold. 'What can I do, what can I do?'

'Nothing at all,' Ben told her.

'Do you really mean you'd let all this go unresolved?' I exploded, aware of Melissa at this moment looking every one of her thirty-nine years, careworn and fragile, so much altered from that carefree Melissa I'd always known. Anger at the person who'd done this to her rose in me like boiling milk.

'I shouldn't think this,' he answered casually, tapping the letter, 'implies any urgency. There are sure to be more, later.'

'More?'

'And every one of them gives us more chance of catching the culprit.'

'Us? So you've decided to help, at last?'

'Later maybe. Can't at the moment,' he said, stretching, flexing his muscles. 'I need to take off for a day or two. Maybe I'll take a trip to Palm Beach.'

'Forget all your worries in sun-kissed Florida?' I said coldly.

'Something like that,' he answered buoyantly. 'Don't worry about it. I'll be back before you've had a chance to miss me.'

Walking back to the house, I came across Dee on her knees rooting out an exuberant creeper that was making a takeover bid for the ground space of the more obedient, if less lovely bird-of-paradise flowers. Even kneeling there in the sun that was no less hot for being low in the sky, tugging out roots and grubbing in the earth, she managed to look neat and collected, her tools arranged tidily beside her.

I stayed with her for a little while, thinking how enviable was her ability to create some semblance of normality in a world rapidly turning upside down, my thoughts twisting in the direction of something I, too, might be able to do.

'No one would mind if I picked some flowers for the house, would they?' I asked her.

'Flowers?' She flicked me an upward glance, as alarmed as if I had suggested snakes. 'Do you think that's wise?' Then she shrugged and handed me the secateurs and watched, kneeling back whilst I moved about amongst the bushes and clumps of flowers, making a careful selection.

After a while, there didn't seem any point in being cautious; my depredations made no appreciable difference to the abundance of the garden. I snipped and gathered until I was surfeited, and my arms would hold no more.

If Dee had been apprehensive, Marian was frankly disapproving when I took the flowers into the kitchen and began to arrange them on a table in the corner. Could it be that I had succeeded in calling her bluff? She said nothing, grimly continuing with her preparations for the evening meal, but the tell-tale splotches of colour on her face gave her away.

Josefina, on the other hand, entered into the spirit of the thing, giggling rather nervously and showing me where the flower vases had been put away in a cupboard, and carrying them, filled, to various parts of the house. Her bright smile made me suddenly aware that whenever I had seen her these last few days she had been pale and unsmiling, quite unlike her usual self. Some quarrel with Emilio perhaps.

I noticed that the cupboard held other things, too, apart from the vases— all the pictures, small breakable treasures and ornaments which had been locked away for safety. Out of curiosity, I reached down one or two of the things stacked neatly on the shelves, unwrapped tissue paper, peeped into boxes. I drew in my breath and took the plunge.

'Flowers are one thing, but this is too much! Are you aware that some of these things are very valuable indeed, Christy? The little horse over there, for instance, is Chinese and goodness knows how old. Those pictures are early English watercolours. My mother would turn in her grave!'

'Dee — '

'And who can replace them if they suffer the same fate?' Dee asked.

I was disappointed not to find an ally in Dee. It was the first time I'd seen her annoyed, or even ruffled, but although she might have logic on her side, I still trusted the intuition that had led me to unpack and arrange these lovely things, bring them into daylight.

I appealed to Melissa. 'Look, I have a hunch that the whole point of what's been happening is intimidation. If you show you're not upset by it, the whole scheme falls flat...'

I stopped. It wasn't for me to offer sententious advice, but I desperately wanted her to do something to fight back, anything, and I didn't regret it as I watched her looking round the room, its gloom chased away, as a stranger would. Her eyes rested on a vase of polished silver, a crystal paperweight catching fire from the sun, the bare walls furnished with pictures. 'I'd forgotten, almost, that my home was ever like this,' she said.

I heard the faintest possible stress on the word 'my', noted a spark of challenge as her eyes met Dee's, a gentle hint that even Dee must not overstep the bounds in assuming too much charge over the house. Her smile robbed the words of any possible offence, and in a moment Dee surrendered with a resigned little shrug and a wry smile of her own.

I went to bed early but I was hot and couldn't sleep, and lay on top of the covers, my thoughts chasing round like moths round a candle. Eventually, I must have dozed off. My windows were wide open to the still night, and I was awakened by the sound of Emilio's motor bike. He and Josefina were part of a local folk dance team which performed at the hotels and *festas*, often returning late at night.

It had grown chilly. I went to close the shutters and stood looking out into the darkness. No light came from the chalet on the hillside, no sound of wild, discordant music fighting with the peace and serenity. Ben must already have left for his taste of the *dolce vita*, I thought, with a feeling of betrayal. How far could non-involvement go? With an ache that wouldn't go away, I turned from the window and climbed silently into bed, but not before noticing that someone was out there on the back terrace below my window. Above the scent of the frangipani, smoke drifted, smoke from Felipe's cigar as he paced up and down, up and down.

*

The next few days passed quietly, busily. Every time I came into the house I looked to see if anything had been damaged, but every ornament and picture remained exactly as I had arranged it, the flowers filled the house with their sweet scent—and yet I was keyed up with a sense of expectancy, almost foreboding.

Now that my sittings for Melissa were finished, I was spending most of the day at the clinic. Felipe was leaving for the office as I came down for breakfast one morning, and handed me a letter. Postmarked Greece. I sat down to read it immediately, not without difficulty, in the dimly-lit hall, while he was stuffing papers into his briefcase. I sat for several minutes after I'd read it, then I folded it and put it back into its envelope.

'Bad news?' Felipe asked.

'What? Oh, no. Two friends of mine have decided to travel together through Greece and Yugoslavia.'

Dave—and Tanya. '*Shacking up*' had been his exact words. I went into the empty kitchen and began making coffee.

It wasn't really a shock, it was almost a relief. And yet I felt an illogical sense of failure and depression. It was time I went home. I was a one-girl disaster area. What had I achieved by coming here, anyway? Nothing. I hadn't found an answer to the problem I'd come here to solve. I had practically given my boyfriend to another girl. I had—heaven help me—allowed myself to be beguiled by a man I couldn't trust...

I had the coffee pot in my hands, staring into nothing, and I nearly dropped it when Josefina flew into the kitchen, hysterically calling for Felipe.

'Whatever's wrong? He's already left for the office.'

She burst into a wild spate of Portuguese, with tears pouring down her cheeks. After a while, I managed to extract from her that some terrible calamity had occurred in the studio.

Time telescoped. I had no recollection of running up to the studio, though I must have done: my heart was beating in my rib-cage like a wild thing when I arrived there. I had no breath left for words—but what could I have said?

Melissa stood in front of the easel which supported what had been my portrait. Now it was nothing but strips of canvas, viciously slashed. I think, as I looked at it, that it was the first time I fully understood what evil could do. The ruined picture, the remnants of hope it had symbolised were as nothing to the feeling of the venom of the sick mind that had perpetrated the vandalism, the sense of violation that hung like a miasma in the bright, sunny room.

She stood passively in front of it, allowing Dee's arm to rest round her shoulders—Dee with hatred smouldering in her eyes as she gazed down at the destruction.

It was Melissa's silence that rang in my ears all day, a gruelling day that was to lead up to the party in the late afternoon.

Almost everyone had tried to dissuade Jorges from the project: it involved too much hard work, the children would become over-excited at the dancing and the fireworks...

He was not to be put off. His determination to hold the party was equalled only by his determination that everyone invited should be present. When I arrived at the clinic, the big news of the day was that Caterina had not only persuaded her father to attend, but to chip in with the expenses to mark his partnership with the American, Mr Halliday.

This unexpected benevolence seemed at first to stun Jorges. Then he shrugged and said oddly, 'What will be, will be.'

With a considerable amount of ingenuity, games had been arranged in which all the children could join. The party was in full swing by the time the adult guests arrived, including Ben, with a deeper tan than before. When dusk was blurring the colours of the garden and the children assembled on the veranda under the vigilant charge of all the staff, the lights were lowered.

A drum began its soft, insistent beat, it was taken up by an accordion and a mandolin, and the musicians in black and white, sombreros at their backs, strolled from the shadows. As the rhythmic beat quickened, the dancers appeared and formed into a circle. Striped shirts flew, white ankle boots stamped, slim brown arms linked, and the scarlet cloaks and the full skirts of the girls whipped round the men until presently the music slowed to a more languorous tempo, the dancers swayed together. I glimpsed Josefina's round face under the odd cap with its twisted upstanding tail.

I stood at the end of the veranda when the fireworks began, near a child whose bed had been wheeled out, imprinting a moment I knew I should never want to forget. Other children were grouped in beds, wheel-chairs, sitting on rugs. Manuel sat with his hand grasping a fold of Caterina's skirt.

The children's faces were raised, their eyes round as they looked expectantly into the dark, shrouded garden. Cries of 'oohs' and 'ahs' rose as the coloured sprays of light spread across the sky. Loud bangs, squeals of excitement, the swoosh of rockets. Roman candles, golden showers, Catherine wheels. Bangs. Cascades of silver and green, gold and blue. A louder bang, and Alfonso Duente crashed to the ground like a felled tree.

The firework display continued. None of the children, their eyes glued to the show before them, had noticed either Duente's fall, nor Jorges, in the shadow of the trees, with the gun still in his hand.

After that, the evening itself exploded into fragments. I remember Ben dropping to his knees beside Duente, and Caterina rushing past me so fast I felt the wind of her passing, Dee summoning Rosa to help. And the display finishing, getting the children indoors and unwound, settling them with bedtime stories and warm drinks. Mechanically, I performed the chores I'd learned until at last there was nothing left to do.

Bereft of action, filled with sick apprehension, I knew I must fasten my mind on practicalities. Young Manuel — what was to be done with him? He would never allow anyone but Caterina to take him home tonight, but Caterina was still with her father. I braced myself for a battle of wills, but the little tiger was still only eight years old, and as tired as all the other children. Despite all efforts to keep awake, his eyes were closing of their own accord as he sat cross-legged on the floor, leaning against a chair. He hardly protested when I picked him up, removed his hat and laid him on a small bed.

I was covering him with a blanket when Ben came looking for me. 'Everyone's ready to leave.' He put an arm round my shoulders as we walked towards one of the treatment rooms where they had taken Duente; I felt his lean strength, and was aware of a concentration of inner excitement.

'The bullet went through the fleshy part of his thigh,' he told me as we went along. 'Jorges has removed it and dressed the wound.'

'Jorges?' Feeling stupid and uncoordinated, I halted, drew away from him, threw him a baffled glance. 'Ben—I don't understand.'

'I think you may be going to.'

Melissa, Dee and Felipe waited in the corridor outside the room, in the driftless way all people wait in hospitals. In the last hour, I'd almost forgotten the terrible thing that had happened this morning, my own reaction to it, but Melissa came straight up to me, and took my face in both her hands, absolving me from words I didn't possess, I leaned against her and silently begged her forgiveness.

The door opened and Jorges appeared. Lines of fatigue and stress had dragged his face into a mask. He spoke in a low voice, 'My friends—what is there to say? *Por favor* — please to step inside.' He gestured us into the room where Duente lay, propped up by pillows on one of the high examination beds, with Caterina beside him pale but seemingly impassive as ever.

We crowded into the room and Ben leaned against the door as if he thought no one should be allowed to leave. Dee and Melissa took the two vacant chairs. Felipe and I perched on the edges of a large laundry basket. Jorges walked over to Duente and felt his pulse, and as he laid her father's hand down, Caterina gently picked it up and she and Jorges exchanged a long and speaking look. He turned abruptly away and dropped heavily on to the end of the bed, his head sunk on his chest. '*Deus*,' he said softly, 'I meant to kill him. I meant to kill you, Duente ... but even that I could not do.'

'But I could have you thrown into the *prisao* for it,' Duente grated.

'I am in your hands.'

Something like a smile appeared unpleasantly across the other's heavy countenance. 'As you say,' he agreed, 'you are in my hands. I knew it was but a matter of time, but I am a patient man, patient and determined, am I not, Senhora Battista?' Melissa gave a quick, nervous look round the room, like a startled hare. Then her breath released in a long shuddering sigh. 'Patient? I'll give you that, but you can be as determined as you wish, it won't make any difference. Whatever you do, however many blackmail letters you choose to send, I could never sell you the house.'

There followed a moment of intense silence. I heard Dee's indrawn breath, saw her knuckles whiten as she grasped her chair arm.

Duente lifted his hooded eyes to regard Melissa sardonically. 'Senhora, I am a man of business, not a criminal—' he paused briefly—'neither a fool. Blackmail letters?' He wafted a huge hand in derision. 'You think I have no better methods than that?'

'You dare deny it? When you've persecuted me for twelve months and more with letters and telephone calls, pestering me to sell? And when you found you couldn't, you began intimidating me, arranging for someone, bribing them no doubt, to play malicious tricks on me so that I should be afraid to stay, and now—my painting...' Her voice faltered.

'Is she mad?' Duente demanded of the room at large.

Jorges, roused from his lethargy, was looking at Melissa with slow understanding. 'But he told me that you had promised to sell to him—and this is not so, eh?'

She shook her head, and he swung round to Duente. 'Therefore not mad at all, Senhor! I wish only that her husband had been as sane—or had the same courage to resist you.'

'Felipe Battista?' Duente's lip curled. I stole a glance at Felipe's face. He was sweating slightly, but impassive.

'Do not joke, senhor!' Jorges flashed. 'Oliver Newman is the man I speak of. He had already promised his house, had he not? For the same reason—forgive me, Melissa—that he deceived me.'

'No need to apologise. How did he deceive you?'

'A long story!' He focused his gaze on a picture of St Francis feeding the birds, hanging over the bed, and after a while he said, 'We have made an agreement when I was looking to start my clinic, an agreement between friends. He had just had a piece of luck, big money, and I was desperate to buy this house. I have a little means, enough to run the clinic, you understand, but I did not have the capital to buy and equip it. It was a matter of trust, between friends,' he repeated, 'when he agreed to a loan, with my clinic as security. He promised me, and I was perfectly pleased. Every month, I kept my promise to repay, a little. Until he died.' He added, after a painful pause, 'And then I found the man to whom I owed the money was now Senhor Duente. Before he died, Oliver had transferred the loan to him.'

Melissa shrugged, unsurprised.

'He had lost money he did not have, at the Casino, Senhora,' Duente broke in drily.

I looked from one to the other, trying to make some sort of sense of it all. It was as though everyone held a separate piece of one of those Chinese puzzles—and one alone had the part which was the key, which would enable all the others to click and slide together smoothly.

Ben spoke to Duente. He leaned back against the door, arms folded, looking tough and immovable. 'So after Oliver's death, you began to press Jorges for the entire payment, is that it? Threatening to foreclose on the mortgage if he did not? Knowing he couldn't.'

Jorges supported this, with bitter resignation. 'He threatened to take possession of my clinic. Is there any need to say what this has meant to me? What drove me to try and kill him? I must have been mad, I am now deeply ashamed, but my only thought was that never could I hope to repay the whole loan at once.'

'Exactly what you were gambling on, wasn't it, Duente? You didn't want the money, you wanted the clinic. It must have been galling for you when Oliver died without having signed the agreement he made with you over his house. Was his part of the deal to be the house, plus a cash investment in the scheme? Was that why he tried to raise money in America?'

'These are not matters for public concern,' Duente broke in, his breathing heavy. 'Of no concern at all to you, my friend.'

'On the contrary. You want the clinic, presumably with Jorges and the children out of it. You want Melissa's house, minus Melissa. That, for various reasons, concerns me very much. Why do you want them so badly is what I have been asking myself!'

'I repeat, I do not discuss my business in public.'

'Then perhaps we should discuss it without you.'

'*Papa*,' Caterina said suddenly, 'I at least have a right to know.'

Her father waved his hand, gave a grunt and slumped against the pillows. His face was the colour of clay, perspiration stood on his brow. Jorges leapt up to hover over him, but Duente warded off his ministrations with an arm lifted as against a blow.

There was a movement beside me and Dee stood up, saying briskly, 'Senhor Duente is in no condition to stand all this. I guess we'd do better to leave it until we're all in a calmer frame of mind.'

Dee, so sensible and composed, always able to take the heat out of a fraught situation—but in that moment I could have brained her.

'One moment.'

The voice was Felipe's. 'I think, no. Not when there is business unfinished.' He looked his usual unhurried self, only the fractional slip of his precise English revealing some underlying emotion.

'But Senhor Duente … ' Dee began again.

'Senhor Duente is not on his deathbed yet.' Momentarily Felipe's eyes were hard, shining like lumps of coal as he looked at the man propped up on the bed. 'Well able to tell us why he wants these properties so badly— my wife's and that of our friend Jorges.'

Dee shrugged and sat down again; Duente closed his eyes, abdicating responsibility. After a moment, Ben said, 'Can't you imagine, Felipe?'

'I would rather someone told me.'

Melissa was frighteningly pale, her skin almost transparent. 'Does it have to be spelt out? We all know there's only one reason anyone would want to acquire land around here.'

Everyone but me. So much was still unclear. The whole scene, compounded of half-understood statements and innuendo, frustrated me. Once again I had the feeling that they were all in it, their secrets sealed from me. 'What reason? What scheme?' I asked.

No one answered me until at last Dee, with an air of having come to a decision, spoke. 'They were going to build a holiday complex,' she said. Melissa gave her a long, startled look as she went on, 'A block of self-catering flats or villas on the site of the clinic, shops where the Duente house stands, a courtesy bus to run the visitors to and from Funchal. For, of course, the Quinta with those beautiful gardens my mother created, and its natural swimming pool, was an ideal site for a luxury hotel.'

She sat up very straight while she spoke and looked at no one. Into the silence that fell when she had finished, Duente said, 'Miss Newman, you have made good use of your position of trust as my secretary.'

'Of course I took the position on purpose,' she said coolly, 'in order to find out what you had been up to with my father.'

'So. But why speak of it in the past? You seem to forget I have acquired a new associate, Mr Halliday, who is prepared to invest considerable capital in the enterprise.'

'I wouldn't bank on it,' Ben said. 'Where d'you think I've been these last few days? How do you think I found out about your plans? I flew to America and spent some time with your Mr Halliday. I don't think he's so keen on the proposition now he knows the extent of the opposition. He's more interested in investing in a plantation,' he said with a glance at Felipe.

'Then I shall find someone else. I shall foreclose on the clinic, and as for your husband's affairs, Senhora Battista—well, we shall see. If I am not mistaken, you will eventually be forced to sell.'

'I don't believe it!' Caterina jumped up, knocking over her chair. '*Papa*, I don't believe you would turn Jorges from his clinic!'

'Caterina, there are other houses. He should—he would...' In his agitation, Duente's English defeated him and he resorted to his own language, but Caterina interrupted him by bursting into loud, noisy sobs, turning away from him. In one stride Jorges had crossed the room and taken her into his arms. She clung to him and he stroked the glossy black hair, looking as if the sun had come out in the middle of a snowstorm.

When she had quietened a little, Melissa said, smiling tightly, 'Don't worry, Caterina, it won't ever happen. The scheme wouldn't be much use without the Quinta and its grounds, and I think I can say definitely that they won't be for sale.'

Felipe gave her a narrowed look. 'It would be a good investment. Or are you so fond of this house, *querida*, that you could not bear to let it go?'

'*Fond* of it?' she laughed shortly. 'I don't particularly like the idea of the landscape being spoiled, but it's not that...' She looked down at the floor, unable to face him.

'Because it's not yours to sell, eh?'

At that she did raise her eyes, huge in her delicately drawn face. 'Felipe? You—knew?'

'I am not the fool I appear to some people.' His eyes flickered to Duente, his breath released itself in a sigh. 'I use my eyes and ears. I knew the terms of Oliver's will, yet you gave me a very large sum just after we married. The only way you could have realised it was—by selling the house. So, I made it my business to find out the new owner. You sold the house a year ago to my cousin Ben, did you not?'

*

I looked at my watch, shook it and put it to my ear. It was still ticking and unbelievably, after all that had happened, it wasn't yet nine o'clock.

We had been down from the clinic for half an hour and the house was as quiet as the graveyard. As I came downstairs, I saw Josefina, changed from her dancing clothes, rush out of the house, her handkerchief to her face as if she were crying, and disappear down the drive.

'What's the matter with Josefina?' I asked Marian, meeting her coming from the dining-room.

'Oh, nothing. I have a flask of soup and some sandwiches in there for anybody who wants them,' she said. 'And coffee in the percolator.'

Sandwiches? I could have eaten nothing, but I thanked her and said I might have something later. She threw me one of her hostile, suspicious looks, then she said,

'Senhor Battista's told me what happened at the clinic.'

She stood in the doorway of the sitting-room while I switched on the light. Her gaze wandered round the newly-furbished, flower-filled room, and I said, 'It looks better, doesn't it? Such a pity to keep all these pretty things locked away.'

Her pale blue eyes swivelled sharply back at me. 'They'll go the same way as the rest—you've heard what happened to that picture of you she was doing?'

I nodded, sickened at her patent animosity, but startled out of it when she said emphatically, 'That was a wicked, vile thing to do. It wasn't necessary to go as far as that. The other things—well, that was different ... '

'It was no different in principle.'

Her stocky body stiffened as her eyes searched my face. 'You think it was me!' she said, and laughed.

'No.' I knew now that there had been a practical reason, other than pure malice or mischief, in the campaign against Melissa. With Oliver out of the way, Melissa was a stumbling block to the holiday complex scheme, in the way of whoever stood to gain from it.

I was inclined to believe Duente's protestations of innocence. His methods, as he had said, were more direct—straightforward, even, if you believed you had a right to batter down a person's resistance into doing what you wanted. Clean, compared to this other way. And Marian, I was sure, was also telling the truth. Jealous and spiteful she might be, but I knew instinctively that she would scorn to lie.

'I don't give a damn about that stepmother of yours,' she said, suddenly coming forward into the room and perching stiffly on the small, hard chair directly opposite me. 'Why should I? She's done nothing for me, she wouldn't even allow me to have my boys up here with me.'

'Melissa wouldn't?' That took some believing.

'They were the terms of my employment when I came here; Miss Newman was very clear about it.' She frowned, rubbed at an imaginary smear on the chair arm, then shook her head as if to clear it. 'But I do care about Senhor Battista, and the last thing I'd do would be to cause trouble in his house. He's been very good to me, he has, and I wouldn't want to lose this job.'

It was evidently difficult for her to speak as she was doing, and I found myself pitying her. I said, after a moment, 'But I don't believe there's much goes on in this house that escapes you. You must know who's responsible for what's happened.'

'I've my suspicions.' Her lips set together again in an adamant line, telling me she wasn't going to be persuaded into saying what they were. She made to stand up. 'I'd better be away.'

'Before you do, there's something I think you ought to know,' I said deliberately. 'It may sound fairly incredible, but there's a good chance my stepmother may be charged with murder.' She blinked and sat back on the chair. 'Oliver Newman's murder. She's been receiving anonymous letters. Someone believes she was on the Pico do Areiero when he died. Someone believes they have proof. And I think that same someone is responsible for all those other bits of drama.'

She refused to meet my eyes, her small capable hands working, pleating and smoothing her pink skirt. 'All right,' she said at last. 'But I want Senhor Battista to hear what I've got to say.'

We found him in the dining-room. He was standing at the sideboard, pouring coffee for himself and Melissa, who was sitting at the table, leaning back against the high carved backrest of the chair, her eyes closed. He turned round, offering the pot.

'I think Marian has something she wants to tell us first,' I said.

*

'Josefina knew who was with Oliver Newman when he died?'

'*Josefina?*' Felipe sounded as astonished as I felt. 'And you knew this, Marian? You knew it, and kept it hidden all this time?'

'I knew nothing—until just lately. Until Josefina confessed it to me. Poor kid, she'd been terrified of losing her job if she told what she knew—her family relies on what she gives them, and she's hoping to get married, and all…and anyway, it seemed the whole thing had blown over. It's more than a year since it happened, after all, isn't it?' She stopped, twisting her wedding ring round and round.

'Go on.'

'Then all this started up—all that terrible damage. Josefina's in such a daydream about that Emilio she doesn't know what she's doing half the time—but she wasn't to blame in ninety-nine per cent of the cases, and that's a fact. Oh, it was all very clever, so that things happened when I was out of the way. But I knew it wasn't Josefina, however it might look.'

'Then I think it is time the rest of us knew the truth, also. You have kept that hidden quite long enough.'

Marian flushed to her ears. 'I didn't know how far things had gone. I wouldn't let anyone be accused of murder!'

'Maybe not—though you did not mind letting my wife suffer a great deal of mental anguish.' There was steel under the velvet voice, and Marian flinched. 'Never mind. Now is what matters. Come, Marian. Begin with the day on which Oliver Newman died.'

'It was in the afternoon, I think, when he'd arrived back from America. He had a snack and some coffee, and when Josefina went to get his tray from the sitting-room, she heard him having a real old row with somebody. Their voices were raised high, but she couldn't make out who it was with him. He banged out of the room, nearly knocking her over, and sent her back to the kitchen with a flea in her ear. She saw him drive off almost directly, in the direction of the volcano.'

'And after that?' Felipe pressed.

'A few minutes later, she saw a car start up and move off in the direction he had taken.'

'Another car?' Melissa said, sharply.

'A white one. The sports car belonging to Mr Ben Battista.'

A Handful of Shadows

As soon as Marian had gone, Felipe strode out to the telephone in the hall. After a few moments, he came back into the room. 'There's a fault on the line again,' he said, going across to Melissa. 'I must get help. You understand, *querida?*' He put his hands on her shoulders, and looked into her face. 'We can no longer cope with this alone.'

The silent communication between them held some quality I didn't recognise. Watching them, I knew there was still something hidden from me. She nodded, and he bent his head and kissed her quickly, holding her face between his hands. He looked back over his shoulder once, hesitantly, then he strode to the front door. In a moment, it closed behind him.

I had been so afraid that Melissa had made a dreadful mistake in not trusting him with the truth, perhaps one that was irrevocable. Her whole action in not doing so had implied a knowledge of his weakness, admitted that she had judged his scale of values and found them wanting, had turned to someone else for help. But now I had a feeling that it might not entirely be disastrous. In some way, the last hours had marked a turning point in Felipe's life, perhaps he was coming face to face with himself and finding he could do whatever needed to be done for Melissa and himself to work out their lives on a basis of mutual trust.

When he had gone, she stood, biting her lips, looking lost and lonely. Bending to pick up Heathcliff who was grizzling round her ankles, sensing her unease, she said, 'I want Dee. Ask her to come down, will you, angel? I'll be in the sitting-room.'

Her face looked frozen when I turned at the bend in the stairs and saw her looking up, watching me.

I knocked on Dee's door, but there was no answer, and when I tried the handle I found the door locked. Going back down to Melissa, I saw the sitting-room was empty. She wasn't out on the terrace, either. Then I heard a series of sharp, excited barks and saw Heathcliff, scampering to keep up with Melissa's rapid pace as she hurried towards the studio—when she came to the fork in the path, however, she took, not the branch leading there, but the one up to Ben's cabin.

A sense of acute danger held me transfixed for a second, and then I was flying after her. When I rounded the bend by the pool, I looked to see how far ahead she was. She had disappeared.

I halted my steps, then I saw her, steadily mounting the rough track that led to the top of the waterfall, and I think it was then that I knew. I raced after her, at the same time some instinct of caution warning me to tread as carefully as I could, so that I wouldn't alert her to my presence behind her, yet knowing I had to intercept her before—before what? My heart pounded with dread.

When I came to the track that led through the woods, I knew what I had to do. This way, I could reach the top before she did. The darkness was total as I entered, but then it always was dark in this wood. Sun and moonlight alike shunned it. It was the rustling silence which was the more unnerving, the creeping silence of night creatures—everything moved in this wood, even the trees walked, I was convinced of it.

I almost hauled myself up the last few yards, and when I came out into the clearing at the top I had to lean against a tree, gulping fresh air and waiting for my heart to still. In a moment, I saw Melissa on the track, somewhat to the right of me, walking towards the head of the fall. I drew in my breath sharply and stepped forward, and as I did so, I felt myself grabbed from behind and a hand clapped over my mouth. At the same time, his lips were on my ear.

'Don't move, or make a sound.'

I could feel the strong beat of his heart as he held me, his arms clamped round me like an iron hoop. I could hardly breathe, let alone speak. And I saw that there was someone waiting for Melissa.

I struggled to free myself, to warn her, but, his hand still on my mouth, Ben turned my face towards the shadows of the trees opposite. 'Look!' he hissed. I stared into the blackness and presently was able to make out the stealthy moving figures, creeping forward, yards only between them and the two women who faced each other.

'I've been waiting for you,' Dee said, rising from her seat on the boulders to face Melissa.

'I could kill you,' Melissa said, 'standing there on the edge. One step back…'

'But you won't—though it wouldn't really matter if you did, not now.' Even where I was, the bitterness and futility of her tone reached me. 'I've missed whatever chance I might have had to make anything of my life.'

'Why should I spare you?' Melissa retorted. 'You have done your best to wreck mine!' And then, with a release of breath that made her voice all but inaudible, 'How did it all come about, Dee? I thought we were friends.'

'Friends? You really imagined that, when you've taken from me everything I had? My mother's money, her house? You and my father both…how gullible can you be? I hated him—and you!' The calm facade had cracked. The cool, reasonable voice was harsh and rapid, slightly slurred.

'Yes,' Melissa said, 'you really must have done.'

'I despised him, and he knew it, for what he'd done to my mother, for all the sordid intrigues he had—even carrying on with you while my mother lay dying.'

'That's a monstrous lie.'

'Is it? Well, it doesn't matter. He brought you here afterwards, besmirching what should have been *mine*—the only happy memory I had left of my childhood.'

'So—you came here intending to kill him?'

Dee laughed, already on the verge of hysteria. 'I came here because he invited me—and that in itself was suspicious enough to warrant coming to find out why. It didn't take me long to realise the reason was the money my grandfather had left me. I'd hardly set foot in the house before he was pressing me to lend it to him to invest in some unspecified but infallible scheme he was cooking up with Duente. And he knew me so little, he actually believed I would do so! We had the worst quarrel we'd ever had, but you of course were so busy with your underhand little affair with Felipe you never noticed the atmosphere between us.'

Ignoring the jibe, Melissa asked, 'Why did you stay, after he died?'

'I saw no reason why I shouldn't take his place in this deal, whatever it might be—and when I found the house was an essential part of it, I decided to make you an offer...I'd no further use for it, its memory was spoiled for me for ever. I assumed Duente hadn't yet approached you, since I couldn't see you refusing him, in your penniless state. But you refused *me*.'

'Because I couldn't sell.'

'Well, I didn't know that. I didn't know Ben Battista had come into the picture with his Sir Galahad act.'

'So you planned it all, hoping to demoralise me and play on my mind until I could bear it no longer. Oh, Dee, all those childish tricks...'

'Childish or not, they were working! It was that clumsy Josefina who gave me the idea, when I saw how upset you were over that Venetian goblet she broke—remember? Your emotions, my dear Melissa, are too much on the surface altogether. You should learn to school them, as I have done!'

Her voice was dry as autumn leaves, and my nerves were at screaming point. I felt the arms which had relaxed round me tighten again. He needn't have worried, I wouldn't move now, nor speak. We had to hear everything Dee had to say, Ben and I, and those two dark figures on the other side of the small open space, imperceptibly drawing nearer.

'I've you to thank for everything that happened to me,' Melissa said, 'even my painting—and those letters. We knew it, Felipe and I, when we heard you had followed your father up the mountain in Ben's car. We remembered his offer to lend it to you that day because I was needing my own—remembered him throwing his keys on the table. I suppose you quarrelled with Oliver?'

'Immediately he arrived home from New York he began pestering me again to lend him the money. One thing led to another, and in the end I showed him the loving, indiscreet note his wife had written to her lover...which I knew you hadn't needed to send, because I'd seen you talking to Felipe earlier.'

'Where did you find it?'

'In your desk,' she said, with contemptuous casualness, 'unsealed. He simply didn't believe it. I believe he thought I'd actually forged it...until I reminded him how easily he could prove it—by going to find you together.'

'Of course, you didn't know we'd changed our meeting place. And you followed him, and pushed him over the edge.'

'Pushed him? What are you talking about? He *fell*! When he saw you weren't there, he began to say the most terrible things, bitter, hateful things—to me. I who'd refused chances of marrying, of having a career, in order to do the job *he* should have been doing, looking after my mother! I'd had just as much as I could take. I went at him with my fists and I guess he was taken by surprise. He toppled, lost his balance, and he *fell*, I'll have you know.'

She stepped forward and took hold of Melissa's shoulders. And Heathcliff, his hackles rising, snarling like a tiger, bounded forward.

Simultaneously, the two dark shadows materialised into Felipe and Jorges. Together with Ben, they sprang towards the struggling trio on the edge of the waterfall: the vicious, snapping little dog and the two women, Dee's tall strong figure overtopping Melissa's frail one. The night was all at once full of noise—shouts, barking—and Dee fell back against the crazy little railing that stood no chance against her falling weight.

*

I took refuge the next day in the routine work of the clinic. None of the staff with the exception of Rosa, knew what had happened the previous night. They had been told that Duente had been injured by a firework, and they accepted it, whether they believed it or not. Few of them had known Dee, but her accidental fall from the top of the waterfall caused a buzz of shocked excitement.

It was soon pushed into the background by the announcement made by the doctor, that he and Senhorita Duente were to be married as soon as possible, that as a wedding present, Senhor Duente was to give them money for the new extension to the clinic. Caterina, shaken into making up her mind at last about Jorges, evidently possessed greater powers of persuasion over her father than I had imagined.

I passed the schoolroom, and looking in through the glass door saw her sitting at one of the small desks with Manuel at her side. Writing materials and books were spread before them, Manuel's face was screwed up with concentration as he wrote laboriously. For the first time since I'd met her, she'd lost that look of bored sophistication. Quite desperately, I envied her.

I went outside, through the playground, past the swings and the helter-skelter, then walked down the drive and out of the grounds to the spot on top of the hill where I had sat with Ben that first day, putting off the moment when I must go back indoors and say my goodbyes. I was filled with immense sadness, as I churned over once more the events of yesterday.

Dee was dead. It was a terrible and unbelievable fact. Dee with her amber eyes and her cool, balanced personality that had been only a facade for the corrosive hatred within her. She had acted vindictively against Melissa, had woven a web of trickery and deceit designed to ruin her, but I still couldn't find it in my heart to hate her. It seemed to me that she had been the victim of a chain of circumstances started before she was even born.

I sat there, thinking, and presently I felt, rather than heard, his presence behind me. 'Christy.'

'Hello, Ben.'

He sat down on the grass beside me. 'I was just going,' I said. 'I've oceans of things to do.' I hesitated. 'I'm leaving tomorrow, if I can get a plane reservation, and going home.'

'Home?' He watched me plucking the grass with my fingers. 'Don't go,' he said eventually, and for a dizzy moment I had the illusion of being wanted, cherished, loved. 'Stay for a while, at least. I have plans myself for leaving in a week or two, maybe we could go together. It's served its purpose as far as I'm concerned. I'm not built for permanent exile.'

I looked down over the rolling vista of this island of endless summer, and could understand the feeling. Imagine never waking to a world rimed with hard, sparkling frost, never walking through a drift of autumn leaves in the park, no sleet or fog, no grimy cities, no stirrings of spring after a hard winter. This beauty here was to me nothing but a painted backcloth.

'Three years is a long time—it's given me a chance to understand myself better. Even to lay a few ghosts.'

I took a deep breath. 'The girl who committed suicide?'

His appraisal of me was sharply alert, but there was none of the anger I had expected but learned not to mind, knowing that it was the sort that bears no grudge, a part of his swiftly reactive temperament. He merely said, 'So you know about Trudi? I thought you might.'

'Only what I remember seeing in the papers—the sensational ones. I'd like to hear the truth from you, please, if you can bear to tell it.'

'What makes you think the truth is different?'

'Because I know you a bit better now.' He drew in his breath softly. Then he said, 'The truth was, I looked on her simply as an absolute pest. She was rich, spoiled, with enough money to indulge in whatever took her fancy, and for some reason she fancied me. She followed me around and I couldn't shake her off neither by reasoning with her nor by ignoring her; whatever I did made it worse.'

'That doesn't make you responsible for what happened.'

He refused to be exonerated. 'For years that's what I've been telling myself, but it won't do. We're all responsible for one another—aren't we, Christy? Isn't that what you believe? Isn't that what you've done your best to make me see?'

I looked away from him, hardly daring to believe what I read in his face.

'That night,' he went on, 'when I went to my hotel room, she was waiting for me, half undressed. She'd told the management I'd sent her to wait for me and they'd given her my key. I had a big day in front of me the next day, and I was fed up to the teeth with her, so I threw her out into the corridor and her clothes after her. The following morning she was dead, leaving a note implicating me. I still don't think she meant to do it. I think she meant to frighten me. There were plenty of witnesses to say I'd never encouraged her one iota, but you know what folk will believe about no smoke without fire. Not a pretty story, is it?'

I hugged myself against a vagrant breeze that sent clouds scudding across the sun. 'And that was what made you give up a brilliant career?'

'Only indirectly. The next day—it was at Spa, in Belgium, I took a shunt that nearly killed me and could have killed others. It's a funny thing when you're racing—it's only when you're not in control that you're aware of your own fantastic speed. That day, people and things flew past me faster than light. Being a racing driver teaches you to push yourself, but to know the limits of your own control, and to isolate yourself from personal problems. That day I went beyond it, and if it could happen once...'

'You can't live with guilt for ever.'

'You're right—and I've indulged myself too long already. It's time for new beginnings. And what about you, Christy? What about us?'

I couldn't answer the last question. I might after all have heard it wrongly. In my present state of euphoria anything was possible. I said, 'I'm not going to be in too much of a rush to find a career yet awhile. I'll have a look round, give myself time to decide.'

'That's wise—and lucky. I want to look around, too, for a house, somewhere in the country. Somewhere with plenty of room and a big garden where children can play. Will you help me look for it?'

He smiled and it was as though a window had opened on the future. Love, laughter and happiness. This was heavy stuff. Champagne bubbles were bursting inside me.

'You already have a house here.'

'Felipe and Melissa will buy it back when they can. I wasn't joking about Mr Halliday. He's prepared to invest in Felipe's business, so long as he can be the financial brains of the outfit and not merely a sleeping partner. And now there's nothing to stop Melissa working either.'

'No. What about my painting, Ben?'

'Some day, I'll get her to do another. In the meantime, there's a lot I want to learn about the original.' His eyes searched my face as if he'd begin there and then.

'That goes for me, too,' I said incoherently, but he knew what I meant. It was all very simple, when you thought about it, loving. Gaining knowledge of each other, building brick by brick, like a good house, that was all it was.

We stayed there on the hill, very close, until the higher hills and the distances changed from lavender to sapphire, and the swift shadows of tropical darkness fell.

Printed in Poland
by Amazon Fulfillment
Poland Sp. z o.o., Wrocław